A CLOUDED SKY

Mistress Richenda Farrell is cooped up with her placid sister-in-law and her children while her brother is away fighting for Cromwell's cause. When news comes that Royalist forces are approaching Black Castle, Richenda feels confident the castle will never surrender, but the castle is betrayed from inside and Richenda and the other residents are at the mercy of invading forces. When she meets Lord Devenish, their leader, she realises she has encountered him before, and felt an undeniable attraction. Now she must choose between her home, her brother's protection and a passionate but impossible love...

A CLOUDED SKY

by

Helen Cannam

Magna Large Print Books
Long Preston, North Yorkshire,
BD23 4ND, England.

British Library Cataloguing in Publication Data.

Cannam, Helen
    A clouded sky.

    A catalogue record of this book is
available from the British Library

    ISBN   0-7505-1537-6

First published in Great Britain by Severn House Publishers
Limited, 1999. Originally published 1981 by Mills & Boon under
the pseudonym Caroline Martin and the title Man With A Falcon

Copyright ' 1981 by Caroline Martin

Cover illustration ' Hancock by arrangement with
P.W.A. International Ltd.

The moral right of the author has been asserted

Published in Large Print 2000 by arrangement with Severn
House Publishers Ltd.

Magna Large Print is an imprint of Library Magna Books Ltd.

Printed and bound in Great Britain by
T.J. (International) Ltd., Cornwall, PL28 8RW

AUTHOR'S NOTE

I welcome the return to print of this early novel of mine, though the young mother who wrote it, scribbling away after the children were in bed, seems very far removed from the person – and the writer – I am now.

First published under a pen name and different title in the early 1980s, it was, in a sense, an apprentice work. But it was great fun to do, and I shall never forget the delight of seeing my own words in print for the first time. I hope it is still able to give pleasure to those who read it.

CHAPTER ONE

Bluebell tossed her beautiful head and shied nervously at the cloud shadows crossing the sunlit yard. Her hooves clattered noisily on the cobbled surface. Richenda leaned forward to run a firm hand over the mare's glossy dappled neck, talking soothingly in a low voice.

'Hush now, girl – come on – steady there–'

She gathered up the reins firmly in her hand and gently urged the mare into a slow walking pace. Bluebell moved restlessly across the yard, held in check only by Richenda's calmly controlling hand, the sensitive touch on the rein. They made a striking pair, the beautiful horse with her beautiful – and skilful – rider: an irresistible combination of grace and loveliness. Richenda was happily aware of it: she gave a little smile of satisfaction as they passed under the arch into the main courtyard of the castle, out beneath the splendid gatehouse with its twin towers, and over the weathered boards of the drawbridge.

Only when they reached the springy turf beyond the moat did Richenda let the mare go, to release all her pent-up nervous energy in a headlong gallop. It was glorious, up hill and down with the wind in her face, field and woodland passing in a flash of green, the air sweet and exhilarating. Better far than to sit at her needlework, or stand for hours over the rhubarb conserve in the heavy air of the stillroom; much, much better than to linger indoors among all those anxious faces and worry about the future.

Bluebell stretched her long legs and arched her proud neck and moved with all her ease and grace over the brilliant turf. She too seemed to feel that for the moment the daily fears and alarms were left behind in the joy of the gallop.

About two miles from Black Castle Richenda urged the mare – she needed little encouragement even now – to the summit of a hill, and there at last drew rein. The horse stood tossing her head and snorting, but more as an expression of her satisfaction than from anxiety. Richenda turned her gently to face the way they had come.

It was the highest point for many miles. From here the hills stretched in unbroken undulations to the purple line of the mountains which marked the border with south Wales. Soft and fertile hills, green and lush and thickly wooded, watered by wide rivers and gentle streams. The sun was warm on her back and above them somewhere the larks tumbled and sang.

A rich and fruitful land, and almost all of it as far as the eye could see had for hundreds of years been owned and loved and cherished by generations of Farrells. Sir William, defying the traditions of his neighbours and friends to ride out under the banners of the Parliament, was only the latest in a long line of independent and highly-principled men. Though she would never have told him of it, Richenda admired her brother almost as much as she loved him.

Her eyes, shaded by the brim of her plumed hat, moved over the beloved hills to the place which above all others held her heart: Black Castle itself. Why it had that name she had never known: its origins now were only guessed at. Perhaps some early owner had flown a sable banner from the Keep, or boasted a swarthy complexion; or perhaps dark deeds had taken place within its walls.

But whatever the reason, it could have nothing at all to do with its appearance. The walls and towers were rose grey, as if always the setting sun laid soft fingers upon the severity of the stone: weathered and lichen-covered but still resolutely massive and strong. A home and fortress in one, at once beguiling and formidable. Richenda might chafe at the restrictions of wartime, might long sometimes to escape; but in her more candid moments she had to admit that in leaving Black Castle she would inevitably leave part of herself behind.

And she did, after all, have the war to thank that she was here still. She should have been married by now, to a baronet from the Midlands whose wealth matched her brother's. They had been betrothed from infancy, by an agreement made between their respective fathers; but she had never met the gentleman, or known anything of him except what a rather unimpressive miniature, received five years ago, had told her. Then her father had died, and William come to live at Black Castle, with his wife Jane and their increasing family; and then the war had broken out, and those dear old friends, the family of her betrothed, had declared for the King; and finally the young man himself had died at Edgehill, in the first major battle of the war.

William had promised that when the war ended he would at once set about the business of finding her a husband – perhaps a neighbouring landowner, at present ineligible by reason of his Royalist sympathies. But for now she must remain single.

So that had been that: she was a free woman, and glad to be so. Better a little dullness at Black Castle, where she knew every nook and cranny, than a constant round of domesticity and child-bearing in a place she did not know and might not like, with a husband who would probably, at best, be worthy but unexciting.

Beneath her, Bluebell, restive at the increasing inactivity, made a warning sideways movement, as if to say: 'If we don't soon go on our way, you'll be in trouble!' Richenda smiled and patted her, and guided her gently forward down the hill. Now that she'd had her longed-for gallop, her conscience reasserted itself to remind her that she was needed at home. So home she would go.

She rode slowly now, allowing the mare no more than a brisk trot at most. The gallop had been delightful, but this was pleasant too, giving her time to look about her, to enjoy the fragrance of the bluebells, misty blue beneath the trees, the sound of birdsong echoing through the branches above her head, the gentle softness of the air. Through a dense thicket at the foot of the hill; out into the sunlight again, where the track ran clay red across the green; and where a dark figure stood distantly outlined against the brilliant sky.

From here she could not see who it was, though there were few people unknown to her so near her home. She narrowed her eyes against the brightness, and watched as his arm reached out in the familiar gesture of a man skilled in falconry. A hawk soared upwards, the sun catching her outspread wings. Very likely it was the falconer from neighbouring Eastwell Manor: they did not visit there these days, now that civil war had come between them.

Bluebell fidgeted uncomfortably, diverting Richenda's attention from the man on the skyline. Time she was home. She looped the rein more firmly through her fingers and moved into the quiet shade of a cluster of trees. Emerging again into the light, momentarily dazzled, she was startled by the sharp flapping of a bird's wings close to her head: the hawk swooped low over them and was gone.

Bluebell snorted, whinnied, reared up with a desperate pawing of the air; and then broke into a fierce galloping flight as far and as fast as she could go.

This was nothing like the joyful ride of half an hour ago. Richenda bent forward, hands clasping the long coarse hair of the mane, impelled only by the urgent need to stay in the saddle. The mare stumbled and swerved, but her pace never eased; she threw herself on, on, in a terrible panic which no breathless word from Richenda, no soothing hand hazardously outstretched, could calm.

She was helpless, at the mercy of whatever the mare in her heedless terror brought upon her. If she screamed or shouted it would only make things worse: and what in any case could anyone do but come to see if her neck was broken when at last she fell from the swaying jolting back of the fleeing horse? Her only hope was to cling on for dear life and pray that Bluebell would halt at last from sheer exhaustion. So she clung, eyes closed against the horrors which might await them, and prayed.

Then another sound, above the relentless drumming of Bluebell's hooves which seemed to echo through every part of her. Another horse, following, coming closer.

She shot a swift glance behind her. Yes, he was gaining on her: the fool, the fool, to frighten Bluebell the more by this reckless pursuit! If she had not been afraid to raise her voice and so increase Bluebell's terror, Richenda would have called to him to go away, get back out of sight, anything rather than follow.

Then just as she feared that Bluebell had taken note of the horse behind, he turned aside, off the track, up the slope to the right of them. From the corner of her eye she could see the black outline moving along the ridge beside and beyond them. So he had not even been trying to help her! Illogically, tears stung her eyes.

What now—? The horseman turned again down the hill at a canter, to join the track a few yards ahead – right in their path! A brave gesture – but it could not work, surely, with Bluebell as she was, going so fast?

Bluebell saw the waiting horse, whinnied, swerved – and a gloved hand reached out at the vital moment to grasp her rein. She drew to a shuddering sweating halt, the terrifying, uncontrollable motion ceased, and Richenda bent her head and buried her face in the long mane.

She was trembling from shock and fear and relief, her breath coming in great sobs, the tears full in her eyes. Thank God! If he had not been so splendid a horseman–! She raised her head, the gratitude springing to her lips, and found herself looking into a pair of cool grey eyes.

Dark grey eyes, long-lashed, beneath straight black brows. For a fraction of a second her plight was forgotten, and her gratitude. Something inside her gave a great lurch.

Then her gaze fell on his right hand, in its heavy leather glove, and moved on to the russet doublet, worn but serviceable, the fustian breeches. Those clothes, and the arrogant pose of the head, the strong line of the body – yes, this was the falconer she had seen in the distance: the man who had released his hawk just as she rode that way.

She pulled herself upright, her head held high.

'I must thank you,' she said coolly. 'I see you are at least as fine a horseman as you are a falconer – better, perhaps, or you would not otherwise fly your birds near a spirited horse.' In spite of herself her voice trembled, and she could see that her hands were shaking. She longed to dismount.

The man's eyes were cold, his wide mouth set in a hard line.

'If you're such a damn' fool as to ride an ill-tempered brute like that, don't blame me! That's no horse for a lady, and if you can't see it you're as witless as you are spoilt.'

The last traces of shock retreated before her anger.

'How dare you! What right have you to speak to me so? It is all your fault! Why didn't you keep your stupid hawk under control? You should have had more sense- even a quiet horse would have been frightened by that! What would you have said if I'd broken my neck because of you?'

'That you had got no more than you deserved,' he returned acidly.

The colour rose in Richenda's cheeks.

'If it wasn't for you I'd be home safely by now. I can manage this horse as well as anyone – you had no right to frighten her so, even less to speak to me as you do! How dare you? I do not think you can know who I am. I could have you punished for your insolence!'

She saw his eyes flash briefly with a terrifying light. She thought for a moment that he was about to strike her: she saw his gloved fist clench on the rein. Then all at once the eyes were veiled, expressionless, and in some indefinable way the arrogance had fallen away from him: or most of it.

'I beg your pardon, Mistress Farrell,' he said very stiffly, as if it hurt. 'Let me accompany you home.'

He knew her, then, but that was hardly surprising; far less surprising than his manner towards her. She sat stupidly gazing at him, as if she did not understand. She felt bewildered, disturbed by his new respectful tone as much as by the blatant disrespect which had gone before. And she felt suddenly very weary, very shaken, and longed to be safe at home.

She was very close to tears, but she would not weep before this man. She bit her lip resolutely, held up her head, and said in a voice which sounded sharp-edged because she would not allow it to be tearful: 'Very well. Let us go.'

'One moment, Mistress Farrell.' The man's hand was again laid imperiously upon Bluebell's rein. 'You will be better on my horse, he's a good quiet creature. I'll ride that brute.'

'You will not!' she exclaimed with a resurgent indignation which set the mare sidling again. She lowered her voice, reaching down to calm the horse, and went on: 'I am quite able to control her. You may ride with me, but I ride Bluebell.'

'Come now,' he said, with a note of cheerful reasonableness in his voice, 'you're badly shaken after that mishap. You're hardly in the best state of mind to control a difficult horse, however skilful you may be as a general rule.' There an ironic note crept in. 'It is the sensible course to let me ride her.'

'And see you with a broken neck instead?' returned Richenda with disdain. 'No, thank you.'

She saw him colour slightly.

'I can assure you, Mistress Farrell, that there is not the remotest possibility that I shall break my neck.'

'Nor, equally, that I shall break mine,' Richenda concluded. 'Shall we go?'

They rode for a long time in total silence. Richenda was at first too overcome with mingled shock and irritation to speak. In fact, she had to admit to herself that it required all her skill and concentration to control the chastened Bluebell. It was just as well that her precipitate flight seemed to have exhausted the mare, for her rider was far too shaken to control an ill-tempered horse. Perhaps if the man at her side had been more conciliating, less disapproving, she would have accepted his offer to exchange mounts. As it was—

She stole a glance at him, and at once fresh irritation rose bubbling to the surface. Clearly it was neither respect, nor consideration for her mental state which kept him silent. He appeared to have forgotten her existence, riding with arrogant ease, his classical profile clearly defined against the vivid summer green of the surrounding fields. She noted the tanned skin, straight nose, firm chin, and a splendid mass of hair curling dark and glossy away from the wide brow. And those fine eyes, narrowed against the glare as he glanced from side to side, something quite other than her welfare uppermost in his thoughts.

'You are from Eastwell, I suppose?' she asked abruptly, her tone as sharp as if the question were an accusation.

She had his attention now, for he looked round, his eyebrows raised slightly.

'From Eastwell? Indeed, no. What gave you that impression?'

She shrugged, showing him that she was as little interested in him as he in her.

'I haven't seen you before, that's all. Yet you knew me.' Her tone was indifferent.

'How could I do otherwise, Mistress Farrell?' he asked with insolent mockery, and then went on: 'And of course your brother's servants are as so many ants to you, too insignificant to attract attention. Except when there is the need to crush them underfoot.'

Richenda drew rein with an indignation which almost roused Bluebell from her exhausted obedience.

'That is quite untrue!' she exclaimed. 'How can you even think such a thing–?' And then she broke off, the, significance of his words reaching her. 'You mean ... you? – No, it can't be: I know everyone at Black Castle.'

'Except, it would seem, its falconer,' he returned, with a faint and derisive bow of the head.

'Since when?' she demanded. 'John Parry had that post, until he died of a fever at Christmas. William left Dick Price in charge after that.'

'Until I came here two days ago,' her companion added.

'Then no wonder I didn't know!' she retorted, colouring with annoyance and urging Bluebell on. 'We've had other things to trouble us these past days.'

She drew ahead of him, and then slowed a little to allow him to catch up. She had no wish in her present state to ride beyond his reach. When she glanced round he was again looking about him, those keen grey eyes sweeping the countryside.

'What's the matter?' she asked as he came alongside. 'Have you lost that hawk you were flying? My brother will not be pleased.'

'Then your brother can reassure himself. Dick Price has the hawk: I saw her hooded and safe on her way home before I came after you. It is as well he was with me, or I might have faced a difficult choice.'

'You mean you might have put a bird before me?' she demanded indignantly. 'Then I should indeed be grateful that you weren't faced with so impossible a choice, between a hawk and a human being!'

'She was a very valuable hawk,' he returned nonchalantly. 'Did you not say your brother would have been displeased? As it was I killed two birds with one stone – figuratively speaking.'

'Oh!' She was open-mouthed with anger; but she could think of no suitable retort, except to say, 'You are insolent beyond bearing!'

'Then it seems I keep the right company.'

She ignored that impertinence.

'I can't think what made my brother hire you!'

'I am skilled in the art of falconry, of course.'

Richenda tossed her head, and returned her gaze to the road. They spoke no more until they reached Black Castle.

By the time they crossed the courtyard Richenda knew she could have ridden no further. Only anger and irritation had given her the strength to come so far without breaking down. In the stable yard she slid thankfully from Bluebell's back on to trembling legs, and longed only to seek the solitude of her room.

But there, facing her, was Dick Price, her brother's head groom, coming swiftly to take Bluebell's rein; and Jane, William's wife, at once relieved and anxious, running forward to clasp her in her arms.

'Dick told me! – Oh, Richenda, thank God you're safe!' She patted Richenda's trembling shoulders, and then raised grateful brown eyes to the man who sat silent on his horse, watching them. 'And you, Daniel – Dick told me your part in this.

How can we ever thank you enough? Richenda's life is very precious to me and to William. We owe you so much more than we could ever hope to repay–'

Richenda pulled herself from Jane's grasp, rubbing her hand across her eyes to dispel the rising tears, and interrupted the softly spoken little speech of gratitude.

'If it hadn't been for him there'd have been no accident,' she said tremulously, and ran, weeping openly now, to the sanctuary of her room. Jane's indignant, horrified 'Richenda!' followed her a little way up the winding stair and then faded into silence.

She knew Jane would come in search of her as soon as she had done her best to smooth over the effect of those churlish words. And one glance at Jane's face, as she came to sit on the edge of the bed where Richenda lay, told her that William's gentle wife was as angry as it was possible for her to be.

'How could you, Richenda!' she demanded reproachfully. 'Whatever caused the horse to bolt, you still owe your life to Daniel Bridge – and you know Bluebell is not safe. William said only Dick was to ride her, and Dick tells me he strongly advised you against it this morning.'

'I don't like you going out on that jumpy she-devil of a horse,' Dick had said to her before she set out. But Richenda had laughed and gone all the same, though Dick had been her friend and ally since childhood and she had always respected his advice. Until today.

She realised Jane was still speaking.

'–You know what William would have to say about your ingratitude, Richenda. And about your disobedience in riding Bluebell. Especially at this time, when you should not have been out at all–'

'But I was so bored!' exclaimed Richenda, sitting up suddenly to face her sister-in-law.

Jane sighed with exasperation. Here they were in the middle of a terrible war, which divided friend from friend and neighbour from neighbour; and Richenda was bored! She looked so deceptively fragile too: slight and small-boned, her clear skin fair as pearl even when it was not white from recent shock, her eyes limpid cornflower blue, her hair fine pale gold, falling in loose curls. If only Richenda had been blessed with the delicately retiring nature which her appearance suggested! Unfortunately it was Jane, solid brown-haired unexciting Jane, who was quiet and shy and always anxious. And with all too much reason where Richenda was concerned.

'I cannot understand how you could even have *wished* to go out, after what we heard!' Jane added with a shudder.

Richenda drew her knees up to her chin and linked her arms about them. 'That Lord Devenish might, just possibly, be coming this way? It was only a rumour, Jane.'

'It wasn't a rumour that he took Byford last week – and Wenstoe before that–'

'Byford is thirty miles away, Jane!'

'It is ten miles nearer to Black Castle. And they say the sack was terrible in both towns. Plundering, looting, burning – and worse – women and children...' The sentence faded into a silence made expressive by her trembling lip.

Richenda was too shaken herself to feel much anxiety about what was, after all, only a rumour. She said provokingly, 'At least it might make life more exciting. There might not be a war at all for all the difference it's made to us so far.'

Then, seeing Jane's appalled face, she said with compunction: 'I don't suppose Black Castle can have much interest for Lord Devenish. We're just one little castle in a nice safe Royalist land. While Gloucester stands, and ... and Shrewsbury is ours, we're safe enough. They'll only come here when they've nothing else to do.'

'I wish I could believe you,' said Jane. 'I could not bear it if any harm came to us – to my little ones – and William is so far away.'

'Ah yes, but the war's going our way at last, since Marston Moor last year. It'll not be long before our New Model Army – or whatever it is they call it – will find itself with nothing better to do than march to support Black Castle. And then we'll all be together again, and the war will be over and we'll be able to speak to our neighbours again, and hunt and hawk and enjoy ourselves in peace.'

'And William will come home,' Jane added

softly, with a sigh.

Richenda laid a hand over hers.

'Jane, I'm sorry I frightened you so. I'll not be so reckless again – or not for a while,' she promised, with a hint of her customary mischievous smile. For all that she was, at seventeen, six years younger than Jane, she often felt oddly protective towards her. And poor Jane had enough to make her anxious, without this.

Jane shook her head, smiling.

'I know you better than that, Richenda,' she said. 'And now I shall leave you to rest–'

'Oh no,' protested Richenda. 'There must be something I can do to help– Tell me–' She slid from the bed, but her momentary enthusiasm faded as her feet touched the floor. On ridiculously unsteady legs she tottered as far as the window seat and there sank down. 'Perhaps you're right,' she admitted shakily.

'I'll bring you a good hot posset,' offered Jane, coming to help her back to bed, in her element at last.

A sudden movement beyond the window caught their attention just then. A man was striding across the hillside beyond the castle, a hawk on his wrist: Daniel Bridge, resuming his interrupted activity of the morning. Richenda watched intently as he raised his arm and released the hawk, in one splendid graceful movement, the bird soaring up from his outstretched arm to the blue freedom of the cloudless sky. She followed the careless hovering flight of the bird, the alert figure of the falconer, his eyes narrowed against the brilliance, one brown, long-fingered hand raised to shade them.

'I didn't know who he was,' she said to Jane. 'How did he come here?'

'William sent him two days ago, with a letter. He came on him somewhere or other. I told you at the time, but I suppose you weren't listening. William spoke very highly of him.'

'Did he? I don't remember you telling me. And why didn't William keep him with him? A strong young man like that is just what the Parliament needs. William is always saying the King has the flower of the young men on his side.'

'The young *gentlemen*,' Jane corrected her

quietly. 'But perhaps we're better without that wild and arrogant crew. What William's men – and others like them – lack in blood, they more than make up for in godliness and discipline.'

The falconer moved into action again, swinging the lure in ever faster circles, his head tilted back as his eyes followed the bird's every move.

'As for Daniel Bridge,' Jane went on, 'it seems he has an aged mother who won't let him go for a soldier. William said it would kill her if any ill came to him. It must chafe a healthy man like that to stay behind with the hawks, but it's good to think he is so thoughtful of his mother. I like a man to be considerate–'

'And I suppose he'll be useful if there should be trouble here,' added Richenda.

'Don't!' exclaimed Jane with a shudder. 'I can't bear to think of it–'

The hawk swooped to the lure, only to find it snatched from her as she fell. Up again, above the circling lure; down like a stone; rising again to the blue. Did the hawks never grow tired of constantly pursuing an elusive reward? Did they never give up and fly away for ever in search of some more promising prey?

'Come now, back to bed,' Jane urged Richenda, one hand firm beneath her elbow. Richenda gave a last glance out of the window. The hawk had the lure at last, her talons firm on the leather gauntlet as she tore at the meat. Her brief moment of freedom was over. With the firm competence of his craft the falconer had her hooded and quiet, and set off briskly towards the mews.

Solitude returned to the green hills. The little surge of excitement subsided. The daisy-starred grass lay verdant and still in the sunlight; the sheep bleated, moving slowly into view; distantly a cuckoo called, his full liquid note echoing round some hidden valley; a bee buzzed lazily over the sill and out again. Richenda rose meekly to her feet and allowed Jane to guide her to the welcoming bed.

Much later, relaxed between the cool sheets, soothed by Jane's posset, she lay halfway between sleeping and waking, listening to the distant gentle sounds. But sleep eluded her. The prospect she had dismissed so lightly returned now to torment her: not the memory of her dreadful ride, but that rumour which filled Jane with such terror, and now enveloped her.

Of all the Royalist commanders, aristocratic generals acting almost entirely independently of the central command, Sebastian, Lord Devenish, had perhaps the worst reputation. Ruthless, efficient, and with brutally undisciplined troops whom he made no pretence of controlling, he was said to show no mercy to any prisoner taken or city conquered. Jane had only hinted at what they all knew when she had spoken of women and children: they would find no more gentle treatment at the hands of his troops than would his most deadly foe. Not for Lord Devenish the gentlemanly courtesies which had so often been characteristic of the conduct of both sides in the war. He fought with all the cold-blooded savagery which had marked the dreadful wars in Germany, of which they had all heard.

Richenda had a sudden dreadful mental picture of Black Castle in flames, the children screaming, old Ralph Davies, her brother's steward, lying dead upon the threshold, and Jane and herself left to the mercy of the pitiless soldiers.

And then she remembered Daniel Bridge, and for once the thought of him was comforting. Whatever his deficiencies of manner, he was young and strong and courageous. William had known what he did when he sent this man to join the twelve who remained with the women and children at Black Castle. If there were really any danger, then Daniel Bridge would be a valuable addition to that little garrison.

Richenda fell asleep at last with a consoling amendment made to her horrifying vision: Daniel Bridge arriving upon the dreadful scene in the nick of time to rescue the entire Farrell household from a fate worse than death.

CHAPTER TWO

Whatever her thoughts on falling asleep, Richenda found little comfort in her dreams. They were haunted by tangled nightmares of flight and terror, in which the insolently disdainful eyes of Daniel Bridge served only to add to her sense of panic and danger. He came now not as a rescuer, but as an indefinable threat.

In her many wakeful moments it was, if anything, worse. She seemed compelled to relive every cruelly vivid detail of her ordeal, unable to find any comfort in the memory of that firm hand on the rein, the ending of the headlong flight. She saw, too, the sudden frightening flash of anger, the disturbing penetration of those grey eyes, and faced the humiliating knowledge that he despised her for her recklessness. It was only as the dawn light began to steal into her room that she fell at last into a deep untroubled sleep.

She woke late, well into the morning, with the busy sounds of the day already reaching her. She did not really feel very much better for her sleep: it was clear that yesterday's accident had shaken her more than she had thought at the time.

She ate little breakfast, though Jane herself brought it to her with what was meant to be soothing attentiveness. The household had been awake earlier than usual, she heard, for though the castle's defences were sound there was much to be done if they were to be ready to face a possible siege. Ralph Davies had been up since before dawn to supervise the work. Richenda sensed that Jane's nerves were stretched to breaking point in the face of this danger, though she kept her fears from the younger girl, out of concern for her invalid state.

Perhaps it was to try to forget the menace from outside that Jane turned her attention to Richenda instead. At intervals during the morning she came with hot possets and tempting dishes, urging rest, and constantly asking after Richenda's wellbeing as if she were seriously ill. A morning of such treatment was almost more than Richenda could bear. In her present state she felt that cheerful, sensible company was what she needed, not this attentive solicitude, the hushed voice and the over warm fireside.

In the end, after dinner, she remembered how Dick had always taught her that after a fall she should take care to ride again as soon as possible: it was the only way, he said, to be sure that one did not lose one's nerve. It might not have been a fall, but she was sure his dictum would apply to yesterday's incident. The very fact that even the thought of the stables brought an unwelcome feeling of nausea only underlined the wisdom of his words. She would steal herself to go through with the ordeal.

She said nothing to Jane, of course, hinting only that she might possibly go and have a rest on her bed; and set off in search of Dick.

Despite the vigorous bustle of purposeful activity about the castle the stable yard was deserted, but for three pigeons, pecking in the dust, and the stable cat, stretched out in the sun. Richenda was almost tempted to tell herself that Dick could not be found, and return to Jane's ministrations.

But he would be somewhere about, she was almost sure, and it would be cowardly to turn round now. She crossed the yard and forced herself to pause and stroke Bluebell's finebred nose, extended over the door of her stall, and talk to her with a calmness she was far from feeling. Then she heard Dick's voice, some way off, talking quietly. She left Bluebell with a final relieved pat and followed the sound to the neighbouring stalls, where the quieter horses were housed, and the children's ponies.

At the far end, beneath the hayloft, was an empty stall. Dick leant against it, talking to someone she could not see, but he fell silent as Richenda came nearer. He looked almost as though he did not welcome her intrusion – and after all, she had gone against his advice yesterday, so perhaps he had reason to be a little angry with her.

She smiled winningly, and approached him, ready to make her peace and show how closely, in future, she would follow his advice. And then she saw that the occupant of the empty stall was Daniel Bridge, sitting on an upturned bucket, gnawing, at a chicken bone. For a moment her eyes were held by the slender strength of his brown fingers holding the bone, the poise of the head bent to eat: astonishing that anyone could perform so humble an act with so much grace.

And then irritation came to the fore. Why, whichever way she turned, must he always be there under her feet, in her way, even in her dreams! She saw him raise his eyes to her face with all the insolent disrespect of yesterday, and her customary courtesy deserted her.

'Do you consider yourself too good for the servants' hall, Daniel Bridge, that you have to eat here?'

She wished it unsaid almost as soon as she had finished speaking: the more so when Dick broke in, and she remembered that he must have heard her.

'Daniel's been busy all morning with a sick hawk, and missed his dinner.' His tone

was quiet but severe, thoroughly disapproving. And before she could say
anything to put matters right, he had walked
away.

She turned then to Daniel with an apology
half-formed on her lips, but he had risen to
his feet and taken a step or two towards her,
and there was such a look of repressed fury
in his eyes that she retreated before him,
putting up a hand as if to ward off a blow.

But it did not come. For a moment or two
nothing happened at all. He faced her, his
eyes darkened with anger, motionless and
grimly silent, and Richenda waited, with
beating heart, where she had shrunk back
against the wall.

And then all at once, as they had been
yesterday, the grey eyes were all respectful
detachment, the proud head a little bent, as
if in deference to her position as a member
of William's family. When he spoke Daniel's
voice was quiet and polite, and carefully
unemotional.

'I trust you have recovered fully from your
fright, Mistress Farrell,' he said.

The change so astonished her that she

stammered a little in replying.

'Y ... Yes, I ... I thank you, Daniel Bridge,' she said slowly, colouring a little as she remembered how rude she had been to him just now. After all, he had saved her life yesterday, however insufferable his manner might have been at the time. She owed him at least the courtesy she would have shown to any other servant. With an effort, she managed a little smile.

'I am most grateful to you,' she continued, and tried not to see the little flicker of disbelief in his eyes at her words. 'I must go and see Dick now,' she added. 'Good day to you.'

She turned away with an uncomfortable awareness of his relentless scrutiny upon her, and made her way out into the sunlight. Dick was crossing the yard with a pitchfork of hay for one of the horses: he glanced at her very briefly, and then deliberately looked away. Full of compunction, Richenda ran to him.

'Dick,' she said, sweetly, 'I want to follow your good advice now and ride again, so I don't lose my nerve after yesterday.'

Dick flung the hay down in a neighbouring stall without looking at her, and said gruffly: 'You're not riding alone, after yesterday.'

'Then you shall come with me,' she persisted coaxingly. With a quiver of irritation she saw that Daniel Bridge had followed her as far as the stable doorway, and was listening unashamedly to the conversation.

'That I shan't, Mistress Richenda,' Dick said firmly. 'I've work to do here. We haven't all got time to idle about doing nothing.'

'Then I shall go alone.'

'No one takes a beast from this stable without my leave.'

Richenda laid a hand on his arm.

'Dick!' she pleaded, desperately trying to win her way through his disapproval. 'I'm only wanting to do what you said.'

Dick bent to spread the hay about the floor. Behind them, so quietly that she did not hear him until he was at her side, Daniel Bridge crossed the yard.

'I've to ride on that errand for Master Davies,' he said. 'I'll go with Mistress Farrell.'

Richenda could see that Dick was as startled as she was by the offer; more so, perhaps. In her case it was irritation which was uppermost. Subject herself to another ride like yesterday's, with this surly disrespectful man for company? Not, she was about to exclaim, if she had any say in the matter!

And then she remembered why Dick was offended with her. If she spurned Daniel's offer – kindly meant, surely? – she could not hope to regain Dick's approval. And in any case, she realised suddenly, Dick did not seem to be any more in favour of the suggestion than she was. He stood leaning on the pitchfork, gazing at Daniel Bridge in surprise.

'You'll not be wanting any one along with you on that errand,' he retorted. 'And Mistress Farrell won't be needing to ride all that way.'

'Of course not,' agreed Daniel, 'but once she's sure of herself she can turn round and ride back again. She'll take no harm. I'll make certain she's well able to face it first.'

So it was on Jane's sedate Bess that

Richenda rode out that afternoon, with Daniel Bridge at her side on the bony brown gelding he had ridden yesterday. Not even the clumsy build of the horse could disguise the fact that he was a magnificent rider – if Richenda had not learned that from his rescue of her, she would have known it now, watching him sitting the beast with an easy grace which drew her eyes that way again and again. It drove any last trace of nervousness at riding again from her head.

She was determined now to make amends for her rudeness; to win Dick's forgiveness by showing that she could be courteous and friendly, even to the churlish Daniel. More than that, she intended, before the day was out, to break through the formidable barrier of reserve and arrogance and find the man beneath – and make him like her in the process.

It did not, she thought, promise to be an easy task. He was riding now as he had yesterday, as if she were not there, his face withdrawn, his eyes gazing ahead. But she was not going to allow that to deter her.

'Where are you bound for, Daniel Bridge?'

she asked conversationally, when they had ridden perhaps a quarter of a mile in total and uncompromising silence.

He turned his head briefly, unsmiling.

'On an errand for Master Davies,' he answered noncommittally, and his eyes returned to the road in front of them.

Undeterred, Richenda searched for a more promising topic. They had covered a few more yards before she said, 'You are not, I think, from this part of the world. Where is your home?'

'Some way off, to the north, Mistress Farrell,' he replied vaguely, and with as little enthusiasm as before. She had the clear impression that he found her questions a tiresome intrusion.

Richenda tried again.

'I hope those rumours about Lord Devenish coming to lay siege to us prove to be false,' she said.

She had a little more of his attention this time, for he looked at her with what was almost a smile.

'I should have thought there was little cause for fear if they were true,' he said. It was said with a faint note of lofty disdain, but at least he did not immediately withdraw from the conversation. Encouraged, she went on.

'Why not? I know Black Castle is strong, but it would not be pleasant to be surrounded by enemies – and such an enemy!'

'You show very little grasp of reality, Mistress Farrell,' he responded, the faint patronising smile growing a little. 'I understand that Lord Devenish was said to have one, perhaps two, troops of horse with him. You don't take a fortress like Black Castle with a small cavalry force. It can't be done. Even a siege would be impossible.'

Richenda frowned a little, considering this new view of the situation.

'But,' she protested, 'he took Byford, and Wenstoe. And Byford is a large town.'

'Indeed. But a huddle of houses – however large – without walls, guarded only by a few brave citizens at their makeshift barricades, is quite another matter from a stone castle, built with safety in mind. Byford and Wenstoe, alas, lacked that protection, and were all too easily taken by storm. Black

Castle has no need to fear a similar fate.'

Her eyes widened. 'I hadn't thought of that!' She smiled suddenly, with relief. 'Then we have nothing to worry about after all! He can't hurt us.'

'So long,' he agreed, 'as there are no weak points in the defences, and the gates are firmly closed. Which is why Master Davies has set us all to work making everything secure. The defences have been well maintained, it seems, but like any good Steward he is making doubly sure.'

'He's well worthy of my brother's trust,' Richenda said approvingly. She was fond of Ralph Davies, for all his fussy dignity, even perhaps because of it. If nothing else, he could be trusted to give everything he had to the service of William and his family. But then William was a good master, just and kindly, beloved of the entire household. She felt suddenly full of optimism at their prospects.

'I can't see why Lord Devenish should trouble to come this way, if that's how things stand,' she observed.

'It was only a rumour, remember, Mistress

Farrell. Very likely there is nothing in it. But the wise man is always prepared.'

Daniel Bridge was becoming almost voluble: Richenda smiled at him with a certain amount of satisfaction, and said, 'Does it not chafe you to be shut up here away from the war?'

Then she wished the words unsaid, for at the personal note in her question the brief animation of his expression faded and died. He shrugged, no trace of a smile lingering even in his eyes.

'There are many ways in which a man may serve his cause,' he said curtly.

'By serving my brother, for example? Yes, I suppose so. And if we were ever to be in danger yours is another arm to protect us. Have you no brothers or sisters to stay with your mother, that she did not want you to go as a soldier?'

'No,' he replied.

'Could you not find a place nearer home, to stay with her?'

'No.'

'She must miss you.'

'One would suppose so.'

Richenda abandoned the attempt to find out more about him. Perhaps, she thought, he had come down in the world, perhaps his family fortunes had declined at his father's death. Yes, that would explain a great deal, most of all his pride: the only son of a widowed mother, reared in a poverty which drove him to seek employment away from home. No wonder if he did not take kindly to his lowly position: though a falconer was a well enough respected member of the household, valued for his skill in a difficult craft. She smiled warmly at him.

'You will be happy here, I think, when you have grown more used to us. My brother is much beloved, and with reason. No one at Black Castle is ever likely to want for anything, of whatever kind.'

'So I would gather, Mistress Farrell.'

She felt that suppressed irritation rise again in her at his failure to respond at all to her friendly approaches. 'How was my brother when you saw him?' she asked next, trying to keep the impatience from her voice.

'I did not enquire after his health. But he

seemed well enough.'

At that her irritation broke through.

'Why do you have to be so surly, Daniel Bridge? Goodness knows I've tried and tried to be pleasant to you!'

She was astonished when he grinned, a wide goodhumoured grin which lit his eyes and set her heart thudding wildly.

'So I observed, Mistress Farrell. And now, alas, our ways must part. It looks like rain, and you do not seem to me to be in need of further protection. But I hope you will continue your superhuman efforts to engage me in conversation when we meet again. Good day to you.'

And with a light touch of his booted heels on the horse's flanks he rode quickly away.

Richenda watched him in a mood of bewildered exasperation. And she had not even given him leave to go!... But that smile, impish, charming, transforming the sombre face ... her heart was not quite steady yet!

Slowly she turned Bess's head and made her way home, trying to order her thoughts. What a man, to be at once so devastatingly attractive and so irritating; so churlish, and yet capable of that flash of dazzling charm; so elusive and yet so very hard to ignore. And why oh why did the first truly handsome young man she had ever met have to be her brother's falconer, as far beyond her reach as the kitchen boy?

Though, when all was said and done, she was not sure that she would want him to be within her reach. Even as he was there was something about him which disturbed her, some sense of limitless strength, of a power scarcely concealed behind the veiled eyes, of something dangerous even. A good man to have at one's side in a crisis, perhaps. A Daniel indeed, ready to face lions – or worse – without flinching; but a dangerous enemy, a bad man to anger, as she had angered him.

But he had parted from her with a smile, and perhaps now she could make her peace with Dick and put Daniel Bridge from her mind. He could have no rightful place there for long.

Yet much later, when she and Dick were friends again and Richenda had spent some time making amends to Jane by giving her attention to a laborious piece of sewing; she found herself by chance passing through the gallery just as Daniel rode into the courtyard over which it looked. And she stood gazing as he paused to speak to Sally, the dairymaid, and noted every shade of expression on his face, the smile, the friendliness, all the light ease of manner he had denied to her, and tried to tell herself that she did not care. And then she watched still until he had ridden beyond her sight into the stable yard.

Even then it was some time before she shook off her suddenly thoughtful mood and went in search of something useful to do.

CHAPTER THREE

Richenda awoke next day with the clear intention of forgetting, as far as possible, that Daniel Bridge existed. There was, after all, more than enough to occupy her. There was linen to be sorted, and makeshift bedding to be brought into the great hall to accommodate the country folk who would seek shelter there, if Lord Devenish came nearer. There were stores of food to be carried in and checked; and vast quantities of bread and pies to be baked. Richenda even found, to her surprise, that she was beginning to enjoy herself. This was not the leisurely activity required of any well-brought up young gentlewoman, but work upon which their safety – their lives even – might depend. For the first time in her life she felt she had a purpose, that what she did was of real importance: it was a new and delightful sensation. And it did almost succeed in driving thoughts of Daniel Bridge from her head. But not quite.

Late in the morning Ralph Davies, busy with innumerable concerns about the castle, spent a few moments conferring with Jane, and Richenda heard him say approvingly how valuable a man the falconer was at this difficult time. Clearheaded, practical, far-seeing, and ready to undertake the most menial of tasks if it needed to be done.

'If he could ever be brought to give up his hawks, Dame Farrell, he'd have the makings of a fine steward one day,' concluded the present holder of that position, with the air of one who had found himself a worthy successor.

Richenda almost wondered if he were speaking of the Daniel Bridge she knew. It was clear that the falconer did not allow his arrogance and disrespect to show in his dealings with the Chief Steward. It was she in particular who seemed to bring out those qualities in him. All the more reason, then, to hope that their paths did not cross too often!

As the day passed the heat grew and

intensified and the atmosphere in the kitchen where she worked grew stifling. At last Richenda could bear it no longer, and went out to the small garden of the castle in search of air.

There was little enough coolness even there, for the garden had been set against the south wall of the castle where it might catch the full rays of the sun. High walls shut it in, and the only shade lay beneath the heavy fall of a honeysuckle, where a marble cupid stood guard over a stone bench. It was for that enticing point Richenda made at once; but in the end she did not reach the shady corner.

One small portion of the surrounding wall had crumbled a little over the years, and on his tour of inspection two days ago the steward had noted that it stood in need of repair near its base. Now someone was at work upon it, his back turned to her, his head bent as he shaped the rough stones with hammer and chisel to the required shape, and neatly mortared them in place. Black Castle had its own mason, but as a strong and able-bodied young man he had gone with William: it was Daniel Bridge who was at work here now, kneeling by the wall at the end of the path which stretched away from her to the left.

Richenda stood quite still where she was, as if all power to move had left her. It was very quiet, but for the sharp sound of the tools on the stone, and Daniel's low whistling accompaniment to his work. He was stripped to the waist, the glistening muscles of his back – at once lean and broad – moving beneath the smooth brown skin, his dark hair gleaming in the sunlight, the fine strong hands powerful and sensitive in their movements. Watching him, Richenda felt oddly breathless, as if there were not enough air here, as if the sun were somehow crushing her.

At last Daniel became aware that he was being watched, and turned his head sharply, the whistled tune breaking off unfinished. His eyes reached her, and then he too was still, the hammer falling unobserved to the ground. He returned her gaze with narrowed eyes, his face flushed with exertion, his mouth set in a firm unyielding line.

Richenda did not notice the colour rise in her cheeks; but her sharpened senses were suddenly aware of every curve of her own body, the line of shoulder and breast and hip beneath the fine blue linen gown; and as keenly conscious of him, of the breadth of shoulder, the bronzed chest curled with dark hair, the suppleness and strength of his limbs, the watchfulness of the eyes intent upon her.

She knew that for the moment – the long suffocating moment during which they gazed at each other – he felt exactly as she did. They might have been anywhere, suspended beyond time and place. No longer Mistress Richenda Farrell and her brother's falconer, but simply two people, a man and a woman, alone, apart, aware only of each other.

And then Daniel Bridge reasserted himself, and flung the chisel down after the hammer, and demanded with sudden swift anger: 'Have you nothing better to do than stand gawping at me?'

The harsh vulgarity of the words struck Richenda more sharply even than the angry tone. She gave a little shocked gasp, and then in an instant her own temper broke under the astonishment of the sudden change of mood.

'A hundred and one better things, Daniel Bridge! Don't flatter yourself'

Whatever had happened to them just before, it was broken now, shattered into fragments, beyond repair. Richenda gazed along the path at Daniel, her eyes bright with fury, the accustomed irritation sharpening her tone.

'Besides,' she went on, 'there's no need to be uncivil because I take a friendly interest in what you're doing.'

He rose slowly to his feet, his eyes mocking, and moved towards her.

'Condescending Mistress Farrell, honouring her humble workers with a moment or two of her time! What gratitude you must expect of us in return! What blessings called down upon your name!'

Furiously, on a swift impulse, she reached up sharply and slapped the ironically smiling face above her. And then stood appalled at what she had done.

Many masters struck their servants, as Richenda knew full well; but William was not one of them. Common justice, he always said, ought not to allow one to strike a man or woman who had no right to return the blow. Never before had Richenda even dreamed of disobeying his wishes, whatever she might have felt from time to time.

Almost, for a moment, she expected Daniel Bridge to do the unforgivable, and return the blow. She heard his sharp intake of breath, saw his hand move up, and then felt her wrist held in a relentless grasp.

'One day, Mistress Farrell,' he said between clenched teeth, 'you'll get the shaking you deserve. And if you cross my path like this much more I shall be the one to give it to you – and gladly!'

She winced under the fierceness of his grip, and struggled to free herself.

'Let go of me! – How dare you!'

'Too much for your pride, is it, that a servant should touch you?' he demanded.

She straightened her shoulders at that. 'No, of course not–'

His hold on her tightened, and she felt

herself drawn inexorably closer to him, until there was only the smallest space between them. She could not look away, for his eyes held hers as if mesmerised: strange unfathomable eyes, full of anger, exasperation, and much more. He was silent now for what seemed a long time, and once again she felt scarcely able to breathe, as if the intensity of his nearness drained all her strength.

When he spoke at last it was very softly, his voice knife-edged with menace.

'Remember, Mistress Farrell, that every dog will have his day.'

She shivered involuntarily; and understood him at last. William had told them once of these wild fanatic Puritans who wanted to see the end of all power and wealth in England, of all accepted authority. There were men like that in the army, she had heard, and in Parliament; and now in Black Castle itself, facing her in the summer heat of the little garden. It explained so much, of course, that she had thought strange. To Daniel Bridge she must stand for all he hated and despised; even William would be no more to him than the means to earn his living, until the day came when all he represented lay trodden in the dust.

She tried to find her voice to challenge him, but her throat was dry.

And then as unexpectedly he released her, thrusting her sharply from him.

'You damned arrogant wench!'

At that words returned to her, sharp with amazement.

'Arrogant? Me? That from you, Daniel Bridge–!'

'I speak the truth where I see it, Mistress Farrell. I am not given to soft words and flattery.'

She gave an undignified snort of laughter.

'With that I can only agree! You're about as soft-spoken and mannerly as your precious hawks – you should keep to their company!'

He gave a little mocking bow.

'Gladly, Mistress Farrell, if the alternative is your own.'

She gazed at him, searching for something suitably wounding for her parting shot; and at last narrowed her eyes and said quietly:

'I wonder what William will say, when I tell him one half of what you've said to me today – and the other times?'

She knew as she spoke that it was a mean and petty little speech, and she would not have spoken so to anyone else; and she knew, too, that the threat was an empty one which did not come from the heart, only from her irritation.

It did not even give her the last word, for Daniel's eyes blazed, and he exploded, 'Get out of here, you spiteful bitch, before I strike you!'

And so fierce was the scarcely suppressed fury of his tone that Richenda turned and ran from the garden, as if she feared that the flame of his anger might otherwise consume her to ashes where she stood.

She did not stop running until she reached her room, and there sank trembling on to the window seat and tried to collect her thoughts. Daniel Bridge – the narrowed eyes, the heavy silence, the sudden strangeness at that moment – which he felt too, for that little while, she was sure; and then that terrifying anger, the bitterness, the scorn in voice and eyes.

He despised her, almost everything he said told her that – yet – yet– He had saved her life – but that meant nothing, for he would have saved anyone in danger, she knew. Then he had smiled at her, once, without irony, without hate or anger–

And what of herself? How was it possible to be at once so irritated that she forgot all common courtesy, and so attracted, so disturbed? There seemed to be no answers to any of her questions, no peace of mind while she thought of him. There was no solution except to make quite sure that never, never again was she alone with him.

She kept to her resolution for the rest of that day and all of the next, turning away if she saw him in the distance, avoiding the mews, the stables, the garden, anywhere he might be. Not that it helped her very much, for he haunted her still, as surely as if he had been at her side.

In the end fate took a hand and solved her dilemma for her. She came in to Jane the following morning to find her sister-in-law deep in an agitated conversation with Mary, her maid, from which she turned sharply as Richenda joined them.

'Richenda, Daniel Bridge has gone!'

Richenda was struck motionless, the colour draining from her face.

'Gone?' she asked faintly. 'What do you mean?'

'Just that. He left late last night, after we had all gone to bed, without a word. So Mary says.'

'Oh...' Richenda felt foolish standing there, her thoughts in a turmoil. In a moment Jane would ask her what was wrong. She shrugged, and turned to the window, saying casually, 'He's no loss, he was an insolent upstart. If you'd heard some of the things he said to me—'

'Richenda! Oh dear, did you have words with him?'

'No more than he deserved,' Richenda said, still without looking round. 'He had no right to speak to me as he did. Servants have been whipped for less than that.'

'You didn't tell him that?'

'What if I did? It was no more than he deserved.'

64

'Oh, Richenda! Now what shall we do? William thought so highly of him, too–'

Richenda turned to gaze at Jane, her confused emotions forgotten.

'You don't think... ?'She laughed suddenly. 'You think he went because of what I said! Oh, come now, it wasn't as bad as that – not really. I was angry because his hawk startled Bluebell – and because of one or two things he said – but that was all. Besides, he's a dangerous man, a fanatic. William wouldn't want him here if he knew.'

Jane stared at her in astonishment, about to demand an explanation, when Ralph Davies came for his morning conference with Jane, and brought the news that Dick Price had known of Daniel's departure last night.

It seemed that long after the household had retired, word had come that the falconer's mother had been taken suddenly ill. He had not liked to disturb the steward, less still the mistress of the house, to ask leave to go, and yet he dared not delay: the message said that the old woman's death was hourly expected. So he had asked Dick to make his peace with Ralph Davies, and gone, promising to return as soon as he possibly could. The horse he had borrowed had been returned to Black Castle early that morning, from the inn where he had hired another mount.

There was nothing, in that kindly household, of course, which anyone could say against a man for leaving in such a way for such a reason. Only Richenda felt a little spurt of anger within her, and that for quite another cause. She was angry with herself for the small leap of delight – faint but unmistakable – at the news that Daniel Bridge would be coming back to Black Castle.

By the end of the day, though, they knew that he would come too late to play the useful part in their defence which they had all planned for him. News came – not rumour this time – that Lord Devenish was moving quickly their way: so quickly, so surely, that there could no longer be any doubt as to his destination.

Ralph Davies reassured them as Daniel had done. A small cavalry force could do no harm to a strongly defended castle. Very likely the Royalists were simply coming in search of forage for their troops and for the larger armies further afield. But they would take no chances, all the same.

There was little sleep for any of them that night, as the country people flocked to the shelter of William's stronghold and took up residence in every available corner. Men were placed at the postern gates in stables and garden, at the main gates and along the walls; and sheep and cattle were driven in from the fields to the great courtyard, where no marauding soldiers could touch them. The clamorous echoing din of several hundred agitated animals crammed into a small enclosed space was almost deafening. Before long, thought Richenda, observing the operation from the gatehouse tower, the smell would be equally overpowering, particularly if the warm weather persisted. It was not long after sunrise now, but already it was hot.

Slowly, steadily, with much squealing of its little-used mechanism, the portcullis fell into place. And then, at last, the drawbridge was raised, so that only its formidable reflection lay stretched across the moat, an illusion on the dark water.

There was a finality in that ultimate resonant thud as the drawbridge settled into place over the gateway which seemed to echo round the whole castle. For long moments a sudden strange hush hung over them all: even the sheep and cattle ceased their noise, as if every ear was strained, every eye watchful, every sense aware that the simple order of daily life had ended, that the waiting was almost over. That for good or ill they had shut out all hope of escaping what was to come.

The excitement, the sense of occasion which had sustained Richenda for the past few hours, fell from her, and was followed for a little while by a new fear, an apprehension, a sense as if of an irrevocable step taken into the dark. They could, she saw now, have chosen to flee to safety; to seek William and his soldiers wherever they were; to do many things other than to stand and face the enemy. But they had not, because this had seemed the only sane choice. And now there was no going back.

And, said that obtrusive voice in her mind, there was no returning now for Daniel Bridge while the danger lasted. She wondered what he would do: go to William for help, perhaps. Or simply wait, since he was so sure – as they all were – that there was no real danger. A chance for her, she thought then, to forget him while he was away, so that when they met again he would mean no more to her than did Dick Price – or less, rather, for Dick was her friend, and that Daniel could never be.

There was not the slightest likelihood that any of them should fail to hear the news of the coming of the soldiers. Almost as the first horseman rode dark and tiny into sight over the hill from the north a ripple went through the castle, through every one of its waiting inhabitants, like a sudden breeze through ripe corn. It was only mid-afternoon, but it seemed hours since that moment when the drawbridge had been lifted.

Master Davies brought the news to Jane and Richenda where they sat at their sewing, though the sounds – reaching them from outside had already told them that the time had come. He stood there with a dignity more impressive than ever, his staff of office held erect, his stout figure framed in the doorway, and bowed as if announcing the arrival of an honoured guest.

'They are here, madam,' he said, with appropriate gravity.

Richenda laid her sewing aside and sprang to her feet. 'I want to see,' she said.

Jane gave a cry and caught at her arm.

'No, Richenda, no! Don't be so foolish – stay here!'

'I'll take care. Are there many of them, Master Davies?'

'Unless they have not yet all come, no, Mistress Richenda. But I would suggest, nevertheless–'

Richenda did not stay for him to complete his suggestion: the tone indicated clearly enough that he hoped to restrain her. She ran lightly along the narrow passage, round the corner, down the stairs through the great hall. It was crowded with anxious groups gathered in conversation about their

70

heaps of bedding and belongings, the only links remaining now with the homes they had left. Then up more stairs, along another passage, and another, a last spiralling flight and into the warm breezy air of the gatehouse tower.

She almost cried out in astonishment at the size of the force gathered on the grass outside – still brilliantly green, soft, patterned with daisies, as if nothing had changed.

How few they were! So few that she laughed at the ridiculous prospect of that small scattered troop of horsemen intending any threat at all to the well-equipped multitude within the fortress they faced. The fact that the large majority of that multitude were women could not greatly alter the balance.

'They must be mad!' she exclaimed. 'They haven't a chance.'

'Not one,' agreed the man at her side, comfortably.

Like children playing at warfare the little troop had settled down facing the castle gate and lit a fire or two from which savoury cooking smells reached them on the light breeze. The horses were tethered to one side, a man posted to guard them, and one or two to keep watch from the high ground beyond. The rest were settled at their ease, standing about, sitting or lying in groups, their voices – and an occasional burst of laughter – clearly audible. Now and then two or three of them would indulge in a bout of horseplay, a friendly wrestling match, short-lived and good-humoured. A little in front of the troop, two men stood gazing at the castle, one a bent dwarfish figure in long cloak and wide-brimmed hat, the other a tall slender scarlet-clad man whose fair hair and beard caught the sunlight as he moved.

Richenda leant on the rampart and studied them.

'I wonder which is Lord Devenish?' she said. 'The fair man, do you think?'

Her companion shrugged.

'Could be. But I'd stand back a bit if I was you, Mistress Richenda. Don't want them taking shots at you now, do we?'

She laughed, but did as he suggested.

'I couldn't imagine a less dangerous-looking company,' she said. 'They look as if they've never seen a battle in their lives, let alone sacked a town. How many are there, do you know?'

'Roughly seventy, I'd say. Maybe not that.'

'Not even enough for a siege. We could bring in supplies past them without much difficulty if we had to, I should think. Yet they're settling down there as if they hope for something or other. What can they be intending, do you think?'

'Your guess is as good as mine. Maybe they've reckoned on finding a weak spot in the defences,' the man suggested.

'There isn't one,' averred Richenda with confidence. She knew Ralph Davies had made sure of that.

'Then they'll not stay long, I'd guess,' he concluded.

'So you see,' Richenda explained later, to Jane, as they sat by the window in the dusk, 'all we have to do is wait until they give up and go away. It can't be very long now.'

Jane shivered and twisted her hands in her lap.

'I don't like it,' she said. 'Why come at all if it's so hopeless? It doesn't make sense.'

'Maybe they were passing this way in any case, so thought they'd lose nothing by sitting down by our gate. Maybe they hoped to find food and, failing that, decided to frighten us instead. I don't know. Whatever it was, I expect they'll be gone in a day or two. They all think so, Master Davies and the men.'

'I hope they're right,' returned Jane, unconvinced.

'Of course they are.'

But as she went to her room and climbed into bed Richenda was not so sure. Common sense told her there was nothing to fear; but deep inside some little fluttering instinct stirred uneasily. It was all so strange, so unlikely, that small inadequate troop of men settling so nonchalantly before what must be the best defended castle in the land. What could they hope for?

'They say he's in league with the Devil,' said that troublesome voice, and she tried to brush it aside. Even the Devil, surely, could not spirit lightly-armed horsemen across a deep moat, up a precipitous wall, past guards alert and courageous – of course not! Yet she lay wakeful for a long time, listening to every sound, and wondering; and trying hard not to think, 'If only Daniel Bridge were still here.'

CHAPTER FOUR

It was there, behind her in the shapeless dark, behind the leaping blood-red flames: the horror, the dreadful thing she must escape, escape at all costs. Fire, darkness, a dreadful clamorous shouting – harsh, raucous, cruel; and the chilling screams of the utterly terrified. Her legs were leaden, dragging, without power though every ounce of her strength was spent on their movement.

Inch by inch she moved, as the horror gained on her, the flames darted, flickered, burnt menacingly low then shot again into great sheets of brilliant scarlet behind and to every side. Only ahead was there any hope, in the grey emptiness of the unpeopled streets, cold, cheerless, waiting for the dark to flood them. For a moment she closed her eyes, but her lids shut nothing out. They opened, and there in the greyness, far off in the unending distance, was the tiny speck which was a man. She knew it was Daniel Bridge, and that he was coming this way.

The noise grew fainter, the flames dimmed, the horror receded. At once her limbs gained new power, throwing her forward in a great rush, arms outstretched in a plea for help, calling to him. She had almost reached him, he was there, facing her: then he threw back his head and laughed and turned to disappear for ever into the dark that now awaited her too.

The flames leapt around her again, the noise throbbed through her head, her heart beat and beat, a drum roll of terror.

In bed Richenda stirred, flung out an arm, cried out and awoke.

Thank God! It was only a nightmare. Here she lay in her own dear room, the narrow patch of sky beyond the window already paling with the dawn. She was safe. Calm familiarity, security, quietness—

No, not that. As if it were the residue of her dream the noise lingered on, less insistent, but there all the same, far away.

And inside the castle.

She sat up, at once wholly awake, her ears strained to hear. Shouting; running feet; a scream as horrible, as truly terrified, as any in her dream. Her stomach turned in a great sickening lurch. She was shivering yet unable to move, her mouth dry. She shut her eyes.

'Dear God, no! Let it not be—'

Another scream, nearer now: very close, full of terror – Jane. She leapt out of bed and ran without thought along the passage to Jane's room.

Her sister-in-law sat bolt upright in bed, as she had herself just now, her eyes wide with terror in a white face.

'Richenda! They've got in! Oh, God, they've got in!'

The maid, Mary, awake too, crept closer to the bed, her expression a reflection of her mistress's in the dim candlelight.

There had been no one in the passage, no sound close by. The noise was some way off, towards the gatehouse perhaps.

'Perhaps,' said Richenda, in a voice which came as a harsh tremulous whisper, 'they're only trying an assault – perhaps the noise is our men driving them off.' But she did not believe it herself.

Jane began to cry, a soft whimpering cry like that of a frightened child.

'What will become of us? Oh, Richenda, what are we to do?' She rocked backwards and forwards, her hands to her face.

Richenda shivered and tried not to think of the answer.

'I'm going to see.'

She did not pause to wonder why she had made that decision. She knew only that she could not sit there with Jane and wait, not knowing.

It was very dark in the passage, for the window slits were few and narrow and the hesitant early light did no more than outline the shape of wall and floor, so that the blackness was just less than total. But Richenda knew every curve, every crack in the stonework, and did not need light to find her way.

Even so she went slowly, as if feeling her way, half-holding her breath so that every sound came clearly to her. In her mind she tried to turn the noise into something else – anything else – than the unmistakable din of weapons and battle, angry men and frightened women. Had a quarrel broken out among the crowded inmates of the castle? Had someone's bundle of clothes caught fire, and threatened their safety?

Now she could hear the agitated echoing voices of sheep and cows from the court-yard, an oddly normal sound beneath the human noise, growing ever louder as she went.

A sharp burst of musket fire greeted her as she turned the corner – running feet, a flicker of torchlight bent horizontal by the speed of its movement, held in the hand of a fleeing woman – they passed and were gone out of sight, beyond where the passage reached the gallery above the Great Hall. No one came after, but the noise grew. Whatever it was, it was there, where the firelight cast grotesque and flickering shadows on the vaulted ceiling – where most of the fugitives were housed.

Richenda pressed herself into the shadows against the wall and edged her way step by slow step to the gallery, her heart beating so fast that it seemed almost to choke her.

'Don't let it be–' she prayed. But don't let it be what? Still she dared not admit her fear.

At the end of the passage she paused, and leaned over to peer round, one way, then another: no one there, in either direction. She slid on to hands and knees and crept across, nearer and nearer to the clamour, until she could see through the carved balustrade of the gallery on to the vast space of the Great Hall below.

Then she forgot her fear of being seen, forgot everything: for the nightmare had come back. Only it was worse, far worse, and this time there would be no waking from it.

There was no fire but the one which burned tranquilly in the wide hearth, yet no blackness dark enough, even in the shadowed corners, to hide what happened down there. The women crying out, the children screaming in terror, the men cut to pieces defending the helpless, unarmed fugitives. They had not had a chance, any of them, sleeping here in the silent hall, hearing nothing until the soldiers fell upon them.

Bedding, torn and bloodstained, was scattered in disorder for women to stumble over in flight, children to crawl beneath in some vain hope of concealment. Whatever had become of the brave handful of men on the walls, only two were down there now, not yet quite overwhelmed by the rabble below: one cornered, fighting stubbornly with a musket he had no time to reload, the other hacking about him with an axe so unwieldy that any nimble man could dodge it easily.

Two men alone, to defend them all – against the enemy everywhere, alert, malevolent, swords flashing in the redgold light, eyes vigilant for a hidden bag of coins, a pretty woman, a cask of ale. Beneath their feet in pathetic disarray, a litter of home-made toys, cooking pots, small homely things tangled in the bedding, broken and unheeded.

Richenda's hand went to her mouth as if to suppress the scream forming silently there. She could not bear to watch, but neither could she move, transfixed as she was with horror, numbed, unable to think or act.

More soldiers flooded the hall, a little knot of women and children tried vainly to flee to safety from another door, but the men were after them; as they went one soldier glanced up suddenly, saw the gallery, called to another.

Had they seen her? They laughed, turned, made together for the wide stairs which led to where she was.

Suddenly stirred to action, Richenda leapt to her feet and turned and ran as fast as her legs could carry her – thank goodness that at least was different from her dream – back the way she had come, back to where Jane sat waiting, shaking and whimpering, in her bed.

Richenda halted in the doorway, her face grim, one thought only in her head. 'They've got in. We must find a way out quickly. There's no time to waste.'

Jane clutched the blankets and pulled them to her chin, as if to ward off the danger.

'But how? Where can we go? Oh, Richenda!'

'By one of the posterns – it's the only way. Get your cloak – and you, Mary. I'm going for the children.'

All at once Jane's maternal instinct overcame all her terror. She threw back the covers and scrambled to the floor, every fear now for the children alone.

'No, I'll go for them – but come too – we can go by the garden stair–'

Cloaks over their shifts the three women crept quickly along the passage, up a short flight to the room where the children slept. Nurse was awake, holding Elizabeth, wide-eyed too, on her ample lap; Jeremy and Robert slept on, untroubled. They dressed Elizabeth; the boys stirred, complained, and sank to sleep again as they were lifted from their beds.

There was no time to waste on waking them. Nurse carried Jeremy, heavy now at five years old, Jane cradled the youngest in her arms, Elizabeth clasped Richenda's hand. Few words were spoken – there was no need for them – except to urge every one to silence as they left the room, making their way along the passage, down the spiral stair, past the stillroom to the garden door. They met no one, not even the guard posted last night at the door. Perhaps he was dead, or gone to the defence of those hapless creatures in the hall.

Richenda reached up to draw back the bolts, and then turned sharply at the sound of swiftly approaching steps. Instinctively the little party drew together against the door, Elizabeth trembling like a little bird against the folds of her aunt's cloak.

'Madam – madam, is that you?'

The stout breathless figure of the steward, dishevelled, night-capped, but unmistakable, emerged from the shadows. Richenda almost laughed, but there was nothing in their situation to laugh about.

'All is lost, madam,' he said. 'We can do no more but save our own lives. Let me come with you. You may need a man for your defence – and I have this.' He raised a sword, broad-bladed and old-fashioned, which he carried.

Richenda left the thanks to Jane and

returned to the door. The bolts were stiff, rammed home hard against attack from outside. Richenda struggled with them, breaking fingernails uselessly against their strength until Ralph Davies came to her side.

'Here, let me, Mistress Richenda.'

Together they worked the bolts loose, first one, then another: ironic that the door should be so firmly barred when the castle had already fallen! They had been so sure...

Richenda turned suddenly to the steward.

'How did they get in?' she asked in a whisper, as if even in their moment of danger the question needed an answer.

Master Davies continued to tug at the final bolt.

'By the stables – the postern – Ah!' There was no time for more as he raised the latch at last and the great door swung open. He held it as they passed into the colourless daylight of early morning.

They stood in a silent group, waiting as he secured the door again as best he could, breathing the sweetness of the air, the scent of gillyflowers. From the apple tree a thrush sang to the sunrise. Almost they could believe they were free: almost, but not quite. Across the garden the shadows concealed the narrow gate in the far high wall.

'No time to stand. Come now – ' urged the steward, hurrying them forward to that final door.

As if to mark the moment of freedom, the first rays of sunlight touched the castle walls as they reached the postern: only a moment, and they would be outside, away from the home which was no longer a refuge. More bolts, a great wooden bar set in its sockets, but Richenda and the steward worked fast

A little way off Jane stood watching them with the children and the servants, biting her lip. It was very quiet, the only sound the rasping of the bolts as they were worked along their sockets. Then Elizabeth screamed, sharply, shattering the silence.

They turned to see her held roughly in the grasp of a burly soldier, the man at his side levelling a carbine at her head. Behind them a third stood watching.

Jane gave a cry and threw herself forward; and the carbine moved menacingly.

'Get clear of that door, or she's dead,' said the man with the gun. Elizabeth whimpered and stirred, her face ashen.

They had no choice. With an aching lump in her throat Richenda moved slowly to Jane's side, the steward following, and watched as the third man sent home the bolts and took up his place before the door. They were trapped.

A little pause followed, a horrible pause, while the three men looked them over, clearly considering what to do next. No one moved. Richenda felt as if their searching eyes had stripped her naked beneath the long folds of her cloak.

Then Ralph Davies could stand it no longer: with a speed astonishing in so solid a man he swung the ungainly sword into the air and flung himself on Elizabeth's captor. Taken completely off guard, blood streaming from his cheek where the sword had caught it, he fell sideways, tripped – just long enough for the child to break free and run sobbing to her mother – and regained his balance. Then he was on Ralph Davies.

'Run, all of you – take – the children!'

shouted the steward.

Richenda watched helplessly as the second man levelled the, carbine and fired, the sound exploding in her head: then she turned sharply to Jane. 'You heard – come on!'

They ran, all of them, in a confused stumbling mass, towards the open door and the stairs, back to the danger they had fled. At the door Richenda, last of the party, paused and glanced behind, and exclaimed with relief. For all the noise, the carbine had misfired. Ralph Davies fought on.

But it could not be for long. They were big men, all of them, and younger than the steward. The sword had gone, the carbine was swinging high, reversed to serve as a club. In one horrible, inevitable movement it fell savagely on to the old man's defenceless head, and he crumpled into an untidy heap on the ground, and lay still. Involuntarily, Richenda cried out – and then remembered too late her own danger.

There was no one now to protect her. She turned to follow the others, out of sight already up the stairs, but the men were quicker. Hands grasped her, dragged at her clothes, forced her back into the garden. She screamed, but she knew it was useless. Jane would put the children's safety first, and there was no one else to care–

She struggled fiercely, kicking, scratching, biting, but they flung her to the ground. She fought on, scrambled half on to her feet, was thrust down again. The hands tore at the neck of her shift, struck her, caught harshly in her hair; and still she resisted.

'Here, give us a hand!' one called to the man by the gate. 'You'll get your turn with the bitch!'

It was over then, very soon. Against three she had no chance. One pinned her shoulders to the ground, the other her ankles; the third fumbled eagerly with her skirts. She moaned, piteously, for the help which would not come, her final exhausted struggles fading to nothing.

'Damn you, let her go!'

A new voice, deep, resonant, very angry; and in some way familiar. The words made no sense to her, and she thought only, 'Another of them, wanting his turn.'

Then she realised suddenly that her legs were free, and her shoulders; that the first man was drawing back, swearing, glowering at the newcomer.

She closed her eyes for a moment in utter weariness. That new voice was speaking again, still in fury, upbraiding the soldiers, while they listened in truculent silence. Then a hand touched her arm, lightly and briefly, though she shuddered at the touch.

'Are you able to get up, Mistress Farrell?' The voice was quieter now, expressionless.

She opened her eyes, and her gaze met that clear greyness she had looked into only the other day – though it seemed a lifetime ago. Calm eyes, cool, a little concerned, but no more.

Colour flooded her face, with relief and astonishment.

'Daniel Bridge!' She sat up, and he reached down to raise her slowly to her feet. 'You've come back after all! How did you do it?'

For a moment she trembled on the edge of hysterical laughter, remembering her day-dream long ago, when the news first came of their danger. Here he was, just in time, like a hero in an old tale... A great surge of gratitude swept her, and something else. She wanted, foolishly, to cling to him, to be supported by his strength.

His hands did indeed hold her for a moment, firmly about her elbows, and he returned her gaze with an odd ironic half-smile curving his lips.

'Does it matter how I came here, since I am not too late?' he asked lightly, and released her.

She stood a little unsteadily, glancing from him to the soldiers who watched them warily from a distance, and back again.

'What–?' she began, and then her gaze fell on the still form of Ralph Davies, and she forgot her own plight and ran to him with a cry, and knelt at his side. He was already cold.

That brought the tears she would not shed for herself. Yesterday they had all been so confident, so sure of safety, so full of harmless enjoyment in making ready the defences. Now he lay dead, and she had been close to ruin, and the castle had fallen to the enemy– Or had it? Was Daniel alone, or had he come with help?

She turned her tear-stained face to look up at him, standing there, watching her in silence with that enigmatic smile still hovering about his lips. 'How did you come? Have you brought help?'

The smile left him, the dark face was without expression.

'There'll be time enough for questions later,' he replied.

Richenda stood up. Near the door stood two men she had not seen before, who must be his companions. Soldiers, clearly, though indistinguishable from the three who had assaulted her: even the scarlet sashes tied over their buff coats were the same. Daniel himself had such a sash, she saw and the identical soldierly buff coat; but there was a fine lace collar visible above it, and his boots were of the best leather, the sword at his waist elaborately decorated on the hilt.

She glanced again at that impassive face, those watchful eyes. The smile had returned.

She felt a little tremor of anger at his

silence, a growing bewilderment which she could not explain. This was not the Daniel Bridge she remembered, the falconer soberly dressed, her brother's servant. Nor, on the other hand, was he the austere fanatic she had thought him. The arrogance was still there, but in some way more marked. There was an assurance about him, a control, an air of equality with herself which had been suppressed before, but had come into the open now. They had obeyed him, those three men, and stood there now like chidden schoolboys waiting for punishment.

'I don't understand,' she began, but he did not allow her to finish. He glanced round at one of the men in the doorway.

'Harry, take her to the others. See she comes to no harm.'

The man stiffened, nodded, came to her side.

'Yes, my lord,' he said.

They had reached the door before that innocuous little phrase sank into Richenda's brain: then she stopped abruptly, and looked up at her escort.

'What did you call him?' she demanded.

The man stared back at her, clearly puzzled, and then at Daniel Bridge, as if asking for enlightenment. Richenda, too, turned.

Daniel Bridge was smiling broadly now, his grey eyes brimming with amusement. He took a step back and bowed with all the sweeping elegance of a practised courtier.

'Sebastian, Lord Devenish,' he said, 'at your service, Mistress Farrell.'

CHAPTER FIVE

They gave her no time to exclaim, to question, to say what she felt. At a nod from Daniel Bridge, whom she must now learn to call by that sinister name, the man at her side grasped her arm and led her away, into the castle, along the passage, up the stairs.

As they went Richenda was not sure which emotion was uppermost. She knew only that fury gripped her – fury, and hatred. It was clear now, only too clear, what had happened. She could replay the whole cruel drama in her mind: the man coming oh-so-humbly to William – 'I hear, sir, that you are in need of a falconer...' – his skill would be real enough, he would have been well-trained as a boy, like William himself, in that most aristocratic of sports. William, seizing his opportunity, hoping perhaps to add a strong and reliable man to the force at home, a further protection to his wife.

Which, of course, was exactly what Lord Devenish intended, for only by subtle means, only by treachery, could he hope to take Black Castle.

They had thought themselves secure, impregnable, and all the time their enemy's plan had run smooth and unhindered to its climax. Their very sense of security must have played into his hands, put the perfect finishing touch to his scheme. After all, he had made his contribution to it, assured her that they had nothing to fear.

She remembered small, as yet unregarded incidents: the ride on an 'errand for Ralph Davies', when she had gone with him some of the way – she felt sure now that if she had asked the steward he would have known nothing of it. Without doubt it had been his own errand on which he rode, with instructions perhaps for his men, awaiting his orders in their camp. Then there had been the widowed mother, so conveniently taken ill – that she had never existed Richenda was sure. And that promise to return, so cruelly kept–

He had saved her life once, saved her

again, just now; but for that too she could no longer be grateful. She was certain, entirely certain, that this also fitted into his design, served his purpose in some way. They were all his playthings, puppets dancing to his tune. No wonder he had looked at her with that little smile, aware of the humour of it all.

Humour! What kind of man was he who could find amusement in what had happened – in the sickening horror of that scene in the hall? Maimed bodies, frightened children, looting and rape and what must be called murder, for most of its victims were defenceless.

There was no confusion now when she thought of Daniel Bridge, no turmoil, no uncertainty. She was free of him now, free of his power over her emotions. She knew what he was, what he had done, what he was capable of doing: and she hated him with every fibre of her being, wholeheartedly.

Anger gave her strength and speed, and her escort brought her soon to Jane's room, where the three women waited with the children, faces tear-stained and anxious and weary. But at least her coming brought some measure of relief. Jane even closed her eyes for a moment in thankfulness.

'Oh, Richenda, thank God you're safe!' Then she saw the torn shift, the scratches and bruises on the fair skin, the dishevelled hair. 'But what have they done?'

'Nothing worse than you see,' said Richenda. She felt all at once totally exhausted, drained of everything but a longing to be quiet, and rest. She sank down on the window seat – the others occupied the bed and the stools – and closed her eyes. She did not want them to ask questions, and even the anger which had brought her here so effortlessly had faded. She closed her eyes.

In a moment Jane was at her side, a cup in her hand. 'Here, Richenda dear. Drink this–'

Richenda sipped thankfully at the wine, and then allowed them to lead her to the bed, where they made space for her, and laid her down to rest.

She lay there for some time – even dozed a little – until the worst of her exhausted reaction had passed. She opened her eyes at last to see the children crouched on the floor by the window playing with a spinning top. She watched it turn and turn in a blur of colour, slow down and subside into its striped wooden ordinariness. Once that would have amused her, absorbed her enough to allow her to shut out all thought of what had happened so very little time ago. But she was a woman now, not a child, and could no longer find solace so easily.

She sat up very slowly, as Jane murmured with concern, urging her not to over exert herself, asking earnestly if she were truly well enough to move. Richenda smiled, though with an effort: there was not much cause for smiling at the moment.

'Yes, I'm better now. I'm hungry, too,' she said. Then her glance fell on the man at the closed door, a soldier standing guard, not looking at them, though his eyes might sometimes travel their way, his face expressionless. She reflected that she would have little appetite while he stood there.

'What happened when you left the garden?' she asked, returning her attention to the others.

'They found us at the top of the stairs and brought us here. That's all.'

Richenda gazed at Jane, wondering how much she knew.

'Who found you? Was it Lord Devenish himself?'

Jane looked a little surprised.

'I don't know. I've never met Lord Devenish – nor do I wish to,' she added with a shudder.

'No,' thought Richenda, 'and you did not see what I saw in the Great Hall.' Aloud she said: 'Ah, but you have,' and saw the astonishment in Jane's eyes.

Richenda let the questioning silence extend for a little, and then said: 'He's Daniel Bridge.'

Jane frowned. 'I don't understand.'

'Oh, it's very simple,' said Richenda, her voice sharpedged with her hatred of the man. 'Daniel Bridge never really existed. He was simply Lord Devenish under another name. A very successful device for worming his way into our trust – and William's – and making quite sure Black Castle would fall into his hands exactly as and when he chose. Very neat, you must admit.'

Jane stared at her, open-mouthed, then closed her mouth and gulped, as if swallowing an unpalatable truth.

'Then ... all the time? But ... oh, Richenda, and we did not guess, not once! Only you did not like him – how right you were! – And how terrible for William when he knows.'

Her troubled eyes became suddenly frightened, her voice hushed, so the children should not hear. 'What will he do to us, do you think?'

'I don't know,' replied Richenda with a shiver. 'It is thanks to him,' she added wryly, 'that I am ... no worse off – I think he will not harm us, yet. But I am sure it does not end there. We come into his scheme somehow.'

'Yes.' Jane twisted her hands together in her lap. 'But I still don't understand. What did he gain by coming here as Daniel Bridge? How did he come to take the castle?'

Richenda was silent for a moment: she

had not yet considered the full implications of what had happened.

'Yes, how indeed?' she said thoughtfully. 'Master Davies said they came in by the stable postern. Then someone must have opened it for them – who did we have guarding it last night?'

But she knew, of course, better than Jane, for she had heard the steward place him there. Her friend, the most trusted of William's servants after Ralph Davies; a man good with horses – and with hawks; a useful second in command to the castle's falconer.

'Dick Price,' said Jane, in a wondering tone.

Richenda nodded, miserably. She had thought there could be no worse blow left with the castle fallen, Ralph Davies dead. But to be betrayed by a man they thought a friend, to know that because of him never again could anyone be wholly trusted: that was the worst of all.

'But why? Why would he do that? He has been at Black Castle for years and years – he served your father before William – what would make him betray us?'

Richenda shrugged wearily.

'I don't know. Perhaps he's a secret Royalist. Does it matter now?'

'Perhaps someone else killed him, and let them in,' Jane suggested hopefully, as if anything was better than to think Dick Price their betrayer.

'Why, is he dead?' asked Richenda, with the same hope in her eyes.

'I don't know,' said Jane. 'I just thought it possible. After all, Daniel Bridge wasn't to know who we'd have on guard there. He left before we posted the guards.'

'It was likely, though. We had few enough men. And,' she added, remembering with a sinking finality, 'Dick Price volunteered for that post.'

'Oh.'

There was no more to say. For a long time they were silent; and when Richenda spoke again it was to be severely practical. 'Has anyone brought us any food?' she asked.

Jane shook her head.

'No. Perhaps they're going to starve us,' she added gloomily.

Richenda looked across at the guard, as if to extend the remark to him as a question.

'You'll be fed soon enough,' he said gruffly.

'As if we're pigs,' whispered Richenda. She saw the man's eyes travel idly to the place where her skin showed white through the torn folds of the shift, and raised her hand hurriedly to gather the fabric together. Jane, she noticed, had dressed in a gown; but then her clothes were in the carved oak press in this room. She turned her eyes haughtily to the guard.

'I must be allowed to go to my room to dress,' she said. The man looked her up and down, without real interest.

'No one leaves this room,' he said. 'Them's my orders.'

Jane clutched her arm.

'Never mind, Richenda,' she whispered, 'put on something of mine. Don't make trouble.'

'Your gowns don't fit me,' returned Richenda: which was true enough, if not entirely tactful. 'And why shouldn't I make trouble? It is we who are wronged, not they.'

But it was no use. The man would not relent. He had been told to see that they remained where they were, and he was an obedient man.

It was a long day for them, all together in that one room. It was a large room, but cramped all the same as a place for three children and four women to pass the hours. They became stiff with sitting, but there was too little space for more than aimless pacing by way of exercise. The children, tired from sleeplessness and fear, became fractious and quarrelsome. And by the time the promised food reached them, well into the afternoon, they were all very hungry. It was not a very appetising meal, broth and stale bread and hard cheese, but it was better than nothing – and it was better, too, not to wonder what had happened to the cook and the kitchen servants in the night.

In fact they tried to keep their minds on trivial matters, food, clothes, amusing the children; but every now and then, try as they might, their talk turned to what had happened, and what might happen, point-less, uncomfortable speculation. By the end of the day a kind of numb impatience had set in, a feeling in all of them that they could face anything if only they knew what was to happen – and if only it would happen soon.

But the night came without that comfort. It was clear that they were to be left here for the time being; and they must make the best of it.

The children curled up to sleep in the available corners of the bed: the adults huddled about them, trying to make themselves comfortable, and failing. Probably Mary was the most fortunate, on her servant's narrow truckle bed at the foot of Jane's stately four-poster: there could be no thought of asking her to share. No one, except the children, slept very much.

It was an unexpected sound which finally brought them to acknowledge the day and give up all attempts at sleeping. Not the clamour of weapons this time, not shouts nor screams nor other sounds of war; but the reassuringly agricultural sound of sheep making their way to the grazing pastures. Elizabeth heard it first, and ran to the window.

'Look!' she called. 'The sheep have got out!'

They came to her side and watched the flock move slowly into view on the green hillside, and settle gradually into tranquil – and silent – feeding. They glanced at the guard, in case he could satisfy their curiosity as to what was happening, but he was silent, clearly tired now and consequently ill-tempered.

In due course an equally uncommunicative soldier took his place, bringing their sparse breakfast – scarcely different from yesterday's meal.

'I *wish* someone would *do* something!' exclaimed Richenda as the meal ended, and the thought of the long hours to be filled came upon her. She did not think she could bear to pass another day in this room.

'If they did you might wish they hadn't,' Jane said sensibly. Richenda sat down on the window seat and gazed out at the sheep.

'Yes,' she admitted, remembering yesterday with a shiver.

In the end they did not have to face a second day in confinement; nor, on the other hand, any worse alternative. Jane had called them together for morning prayers – a usual practice of the household, but somehow more significant in the present crisis – and then they had made some attempt to tidy the room. Jane was on the point of proposing to hear the children at their lessons, as far as she could in the present conditions, when a call from the passage outside spared them that fate. The guard, evidently recognising the voice, was quick to unlock the door and pull it open, and Lord Devenish came in.

He dismissed the guard and stood just inside the closed door, looking at them. Again that detestable little smile. Richenda clenched her fists against a longing to strike it from his face somehow with all the power of her slender hands. None of them moved: they sat ranged on the bed, the children huddled close to their mother, gazing at him. Only Jeremy sat apart from them, on the floor by the window with his hands grasping his favourite toy, a wooden horse on wheels: but equally he did not move.

'Good morning, ladies,' Lord Devenish

said pleasantly, apparently oblivious of the repelled fascination in Jane's expression at this new part he was playing in her life. Then he added with a slight mocking bow in Jeremy's direction, 'And gentleman, of course.'

No one said anything. Even their captor was silent for a moment or two. Then he said:

'You may consider yourselves at liberty.'

Jane gasped, and Richenda reached out a warning hand to silence her.

'Precisely what do you mean by that, my lord?' she asked coldly.

'What I say, Mistress Farrell. That you are free, all of you, to wander as you will about the castle. Consider yourselves, so to speak, at home.'

She glowered at him for that additional measure of salt in their wounds. 'About the castle? But not outside?'

'Of course not. What did you expect?'

Richenda's eyes flashed, as if her expectations of him were too low for words.

'And what of the others?'

He raised a dark eyebrow. 'Others?'

'Those who are still alive, that is. The women and children who took shelter here. My brother's servants, and the other men.'

'They, Mistress Farrell, have their entire liberty – those, as you so aptly said, who are still alive. I fear the casualties amongst the men were high, but the countryfolk and the female servants have gone. There is no sense in encumbering ourselves unnecessarily, you must agree. In fact, if they wish it, the two who remain here with you may go – I am a reasonable man.'

'Then God save us from unreason!' exclaimed Richenda. She turned to glance at Mary and Nurse, saw their eyes meet, saw them look briefly at Jane. Her sister-in-law had not noticed the incident.

'Why may we not go free then?' she asked tremulously.

Lord Devenish's voice softened just a little as he spoke to her, as if he sensed that she was made of less resilient mettle than Richenda.

'Because, madam, your presence affords me and my men a measure of protection. You must see that.'

'I don't,' objected Jane. She was quickly becoming tearful. 'We are helpless women and children. I beg you to let us go! We can do you no harm, God knows.'

'What he means,' Richenda interpreted sharply, 'is that we may be useful as hostages, if William comes against the castle. Our lives against yours, is that not it?'

'Something of the sort,' he agreed blandly.

Unexpectedly Jeremy broke in, seizing on the one point he understood. 'My father will come for my birthday,' he asserted, his piping voice falling with innocent clarity into the tense atmosphere.

Gravely, Lord Devenish turned to look at him.

'Indeed, young man? What makes you so sure of that?'

'Because,' explained Jeremy fearlessly, 'it will be my sixth birthday. I am to be breeched, and Father *promised* to come home.'

Richenda was surprised to see in their captor's face an amused understanding: he too, of course, must have lived through that important day in a boy's life, when the skirts of babyhood were laid aside for ever and the man's clothes in miniature put on with all due ceremony: a moment of celebration, in any well-to-do family. But whatever sympathy he felt was short-lived. His own needs were quickly uppermost again.

'And when, young man, is your sixth birthday?' he asked.

'September the fifteenth,' Jeremy replied clearly.

Lord Devenish smiled pleasantly.

'Then we must be ready to welcome him, must we not? It gives us ample time.' He turned again to the ladies. 'As I said, while you, madam, and Mistress Farrell and the children, must remain, your servants are free to go if they so wish. There is, as I am sure you will impress upon them, no disgrace in choosing their freedom, since all their fellows have done so already–'

'Except Dick Price,' broke in Richenda impulsively, hoping for confirmation – or even denial. Lord Devenish raised an eyebrow, his surprise momentarily visible through the calm exterior.

'Ah! So you know about that. Yes, as you

so rightly say, except Dick Price. You may well come across him: just remember, for your own good, that he is now my man.'

'What did you do?' demanded Richenda. 'How did you make him betray us?'

'It was an unpleasant discovery for you to make, I imagine, that one apparently so loyal should be the Judas within the camp. There is a certain satisfaction for my part in having subverted the most seemingly incorruptible of your household. But, Mistress Farrell, you must recollect that every man has his price – if you will forgive the pun. It is not the amount of his resources which is useful to a man in my position, but what he does with them. I used the little I had to good effect. One man, one well-filled purse – one stronghold neatly in my hands.'

'You are detestable!' she exclaimed.

'But of course,' he returned, unruffled. 'I am your enemy: we are at war. Now,' he went on briskly, 'let us have everything clear between us. As I said, the servants may go, if they so wish. In case they need time to reflect, I shall not expect an answer now –

a word to one of my men will reach me if I cannot be found. There will be a man stationed always outside this door, for example. As for you–' he bowed slightly to Jane and Richenda –'you are at liberty to make what use you will of the castle, so long as it does not interfere with my business. But make no mistake – there is no escape. I know what treachery can do, and I trust no one. Every point has its double guard. One false step on your part – any of you – and you will be secured again in one room, with a guard. I don't imagine that is a pleasant experience. A further point: you will join us daily for supper in the Great Hall. The children only will be exempt from that.'

This time Jane's indignation overcame her timidity. 'How can you!' she exclaimed. 'What kind of monsters do you think we are, to break bread with my husband's enemies in his own house? I would die first.'

'So be it,' he said lightly. 'If you will not eat with us, you will not eat at all. Nor,' he added menacingly, 'will the children.'

'Now I know what they mean when they say you serve the Devil!' retorted Jane in frustrated anger.

Richenda rounded on him. 'What possible purpose can it serve for us to eat with you?' she demanded.

He smiled serenely. 'I shall be able to savour my triumph,' he said. 'But on a purely practical level, Mistress Farrell, I am aware that women often have certain skills with herbs and simples. I do not know what little potions you may have concealed in your still room. But, just in case, you eat what we eat, at the same table. I have, you see, a well-developed instinct for self-preservation.'

'No,' she corrected him, 'an unpleasant mind. We do not all have your treacherous nature, my lord.'

He laughed then, briefly.

'Perhaps, Mistress Farrell, that is why I am here now – and you are there. But if you prefer it, think only that your civilising presence – and that of Dame Farrell – will add greatly to our enjoyment of whatever dishes this castle has to offer. I shall send word each day when your attendance is required in the hall – and look forward to receiving you there. Good day to you all.'

He turned away from them, and then paused and glanced round. 'One thing more, a warning. I would not advise you to walk unaccompanied about the castle. There are some camp-followers among my troop, but not many. Most of the men have seen little of women of late – and you know, I think, what that means. I should not wish to have to come to the rescue again. I might be too late next time.'

And with that he was gone.

Richenda looked at Jane, then at the servants.

'Well, now we know where we stand,' she commented grimly. 'I suppose it's better than not knowing.'

'I do not know how I, or William indeed, could ever have thought well of that man,' Jane said sadly. Then she went on with indignation, 'And how dared he suggest that Mary or Nurse would wish to leave us in our need? I think he has treachery in his blood, to see it everywhere.'

Richenda laid a hand on her arm.

'One moment, Jane,' she warned. 'It's not

so simple as that. I think it would not be right or just for us to ask anyone needlessly to share our fate. I am sure if you think about it you will agree. Mary has a family away from here, people she loves: why should she stay? And Nurse, too, has a right to make her own choice. After all, we shall not have a great deal to do, that we must have servants about us, however much we might be glad of their company.'

'Richenda—' Jane began in protest, but Richenda silenced her.

'No, Jane, let Mary choose, and Nurse.' She looked at the two women, who gazed back at her, unsure what to say. Then Mary stammered:

'We couldn't ... could we?... What would you think of us...?'

'Only that you had chosen to do what I would choose in your place,' said Richenda gently. 'Do you think I would stay here for a moment longer if I were free to go? And this is my home, remember, as it is not yours.'

'Then,' said Mary slowly, 'I should like to go ... please...' Her eyes begged them not to judge her too harshly for her choice. Jane bent her head and said nothing.

'And you, Nurse?' asked Richenda.

'Where would I go then, pray?' demanded Nurse roughly. 'I nursed you and Master William from the day you were born, and all these little ones. No, I'll not leave you until they carry me out to my grave – and that's not that I think the worse of you, Mary,' she added. 'It's another matter for you. But that's my choice.'

Jane flung her arms about the old woman and burst into tears. 'Oh, thank you, Nurse, thank you!'

It was not until Mary had gone that it came home to them at last with bitter force that they were helpless prisoners in their own home.

CHAPTER SIX

It was not until evening drew near and Richenda went to her room to prepare for supper that she knew she had never been so afraid as she was now, except perhaps in that horrible moment in the garden.

It was a painful experience for all of them, to find themselves hostages in the hands of a dangerous enemy. But at least they knew that it was not in their captor's interests to harm them. It was a faint crumb of comfort.

And it was one which Richenda could not take for herself. As William's sister she had not quite the usefulness of his wife and children, though perhaps that fact might preserve her life. It would not save her from humiliation, perhaps worse, at the hands of a man who had every reason to hate her.

She had allowed her irritation at his manner to lead her into a rudeness and ingratitude wholly foreign to her. And it would be no help to her now that much of her ill-temper had stemmed from her sense of his oddness, the things which made him unlike the simple falconer he claimed to be. In taunting him, in losing her temper with him, she had behaved like the spoilt girl he must think her. And now he would use her as he pleased and she would have no defence at all against him.

Very soon the man would come to summon them to the hall, and she must face their enemy, and whatever punishment he chose to inflict upon her for her past usage of him. As she pulled open the clothes press to choose a gown she saw that her hands were trembling.

She bit her lip, and closed her eyes for a moment, and made a resolution: not for one fraction of a second must Lord Devenish know that she was afraid.

That was how she came to be standing before her mirror when Jane came to find her, brushing her hair to complete an ensemble fit for a court ball.

She heard Jane's gasp and turned, her hairbrush poised above her head. A few strands of her hair were caught in it still, curling silken and shining in the evening sunlight. On the table beside the mirror lay the delicate silver chain, linked at intervals with pearls, which was to be looped and twisted through that lovely hair. Similar pearls decorated the slashed sleeves of her satin gown at the point where the white silk of the shift swelled through the sapphire blue. The skirts fell like a blue flower – blue as her eyes – to the floor, spreading out from the tiny waist.

She looked enchanting, fairy-like, her fragile beauty set off to perfection by the delicacy of the gown. So she had looked once at the festivities for Robert's christening, at the feasting to celebrate William's occasional returns. But this time Jane found the vision less than breathtaking, repugnant even.

'Richenda! You can't dress like that! It's … it's…'

The words tailed off into inexpressible outrage.

'What's wrong?' Richenda asked innocently, her eyes wide. 'It is my best gown.'

'Have you lost all sense of decency?' demanded Jane. 'We are to eat – under duress, remember – with William's enemy – a man with hands dyed deep in the blood of our friends. An evil man – and yet you dress as if for a festival! You must change at once – do as I do, wear what you had on before.'

Richenda laughed brightly.

'Do you want me to dine in my shift?' Then she took pity on Jane and became immediately serious: she laid down her brush and came to her side. She had sufficient control of herself now to still the trembling of her outstretched hands.

'Jane dear, I am not so unthinking as you must feel. But I refuse to appear in the hall looking cowed and defeated: that will only make them the more triumphant. No, I intend to sweep in here as if I were the Queen herself and they beggars at my door – and I suggest you ought to do the same.'

She subjected Jane's dark homespun to a despairing scrutiny. 'Look at you, with a torn hem and mud on your skirts, and a stain of something or other on your bodice. They *must* not be able for one moment to despise us. This is their victory feast: we must make sure they are made to feel just a little like intruders.'

She bore the protesting Jane to her room and threw open the clothes press. 'Now, let's see – here, this is better. It's your most becoming gown–'

'But the neckline – I only wear it if William's there...'

'What about mine, then? – But if it troubles you, put this neckerchief about you – I was intending to do the same.'

Reluctantly, with Richenda's help, Jane dressed in the amber satin which looked well with her brown colouring, and gave her an unexpected richness of appearance. She had to admit to herself that she felt better able to face the ordeal which awaited them, knowing she looked as nearly pretty as was possible.

By the time the man came from Lord Devenish to escort them to supper they were ready, hair pinned and jewelled in place, the lacy folds of their neckerchiefs preserving them from any possible im-modesty, heads held high. They even had the satisfaction of seeing the man give a little start of surprise, quickly suppressed, at their appearance.

Before they set out for the hall Jane ran to say goodnight to the children and returned with traces of tears visible about her anxious eyes. 'I don't like leaving them,' she confessed. 'We don't know what may happen.'

'We're only going to supper downstairs,' said Richenda cheerfully. 'They'll come to no harm – and Nurse is with them.'

It would not do for Jane to appear in the hall with that troubled expression to lessen the dramatic impact of their appearance, she thought. She set herself to coax her companion, teasingly, to a happier frame of mind. She succeeded at least in so far as Jane had put the children to the back of her mind by the time they came to the end of the passage, and was asking her in a whisper, 'Aren't you even a little afraid?'

Richenda turned her head, and smiled.

'Of course,' she whispered in return, 'but they must never know it.'

It sounded so simple, but only she knew how hard it was, to achieve the proud serenity of manner which would deceive them all. 'Every dog will have his day', he had said to her, and she had misunderstood him completely. Now she knew exactly what he had meant, for his day had come. She was in his power, totally, helplessly. Nothing she could do or say would come to her aid, no one could save her if he did not choose.

She did not for one moment regret the things she had said to him, even her ingratitude that he had saved her life. Knowing what he was, she was glad that she at least had not been entirely blind. But for that, if he chose, he could exact a terrible revenge. And down there in the hall, with all his soldiers, he waited in triumph, to savour this moment when she and all she loved lay in his power.

If they had not guessed it before, they would have known as soon as they reached the gallery that it was a victory feast. The great hall was ablaze with candles and torches, the tables spread with the greatest variety of dishes which a military force in time of war could produce. Almost the whole troop must be there, ranged on benches along the tables, laughing, talking, eyes eagerly scanning the banquet before them, waiting only for the two captives to join them. The camp-followers Lord Devenish had spoken of were there, too, confined to a corner at the further end from the fire: it was in the throng somewhere at that point that Richenda glimpsed Dick Price.

For a moment his eye caught hers, then he glanced away, head bent, and she saw with satisfaction that he had coloured uncomfortably. She hoped he would find the evening as unpleasant as possible.

At the head of the stairs their escort stood to one side and they began slowly, together, to descend. Facing them at the far end of the hall, at a table set before the hearth, Lord Devenish waited and watched.

Gone now was any remaining trace of Daniel Bridge, the falconer: hard indeed to believe that he had ever worn russet homespun or slept in the loft above the mews. Only his hair still retained its disguising shortness in contrast to the lavish lovelocks of the men who sat to right and left of him. But for all that Richenda knew she would not now have guessed any but him to be in command, for all the fair elegance of the bearded man she had seen from the castle walls. She supposed now that the dwarfed figure who had stood at his side must have been Lord Devenish, ensuring that he was not recognised.

He was not so tall as the fair man, but beside him as he rose to his feet everyone else shrank into insignificance. He was erect, proud, his dark head thrown back so that the firelight lit the chestnut glimmers in that glossy hair; his strong lithe figure emphasised by the immaculately cut doublet of scarlet, the whiteness of lace at neck and wrists contrasting with the bronze of his skin. His long slender hands – strong supple hands – rested on the table before him, those grey eyes, keen as a hawk's below the dark brows, resting on the two ladies.

For a moment, in spite of everything, Richenda paused, fascinated, mesmerised by his splendid presence, forgetting momentarily what he had done, why they were here.

Then she pulled herself together, cursing the fate which had given their deadly enemy so disturbing a physical presence. Evil, too, had its beauty if you allowed yourself to yield to its allure, she told herself. She took a deep breath, raised her skirts just high enough to reveal the silver satin of her slippers, and moved on with dignity.

A silence fell over the hall. Richenda's heart beat faster: even dressed so finely, it took more courage than she had expected to brave those watching eyes, the avid interest, the triumphant curiosity. And where must they go? Where were they to sit? Not, surely – a sudden horrible moment of panic – among the camp-followers? Her eyes flew to that hated face, seeking an answer.

The reply came quickly. With a dignity as impressive as their own and a courtesy which matched their finery, Lord Devenish came to meet them. He bowed, held a hand to each of them, led them to sit one on either side of him in the place of honour by the fire: all without a word.

And then the feasting began.

Richenda did not know exactly what she

had expected. Humiliation, certainly, some clear reminder that they were powerless, at his mercy. Certainly the ironic triumph of the hated smile. She had feared it might even be worse, and been ready to return every insult with grave dignity. Then, she felt, in some small measure the victory would also be theirs.

But it was almost as if he had known how she would behave, what she would do, and cheated her even of that little triumph. They were received with all the solemn ceremony appropriate to bereaved queens, as if they merited every consideration in their present loss. Dishes were passed in silence, the conversation around them was restrained and discreet, the high spirits evident elsewhere in the hall deliberately suppressed.

And yet when Lord Devenish's eyes rested upon her, Richenda could see in them the satisfaction of the conqueror, the triumph he would not show by word or gesture to anyone else. As the meal slowly progressed her longing grew, stronger even than her fear, to answer the silent message of his eyes, to hurt or humiliate him before all that throng because of what he had done to them.

She waited until there was one of those inexplicable lulls in the general rowdiness of the hall which from time to time afflict any large gathering, when for a moment only two or three voices spoke on. Then she turned to Lord Devenish and asked with icy clarity, 'How does it feel, my lord, to feast in the house where you were employed as a servant, too humble for the high table?'

It would have been unpardonably rude to any but the man who had done them such wrong.

She heard a sharp, shocked intake of breath from the bearded man at her other side; saw Jane's face flushed with embarrassment; felt the awed silence fill the room.

She saw too the angry light flash in Lord Devenish's eyes, the colour deepen along his strongly-marked cheekbones. She watched his fingers tighten about the stem of his wineglass – William's wineglass – and waited like everyone else for the humiliating retort which must come, unrepentant, her eyes bright and angry as his.

Then he took a deep breath and leant back in his chair. Courtesy veiled his eyes, the ironic smile was there at last – a little rueful this time. He said easily, 'It is pleasant indeed, Mistress Farrell. Particularly when the company is so agreeable.'

The soldiers relaxed in disappointment, the noise rose again to its earlier level. Lord Devenish passed a dish of plovers' eggs for her attention.

'May I press these upon you, Mistress Farrell? They are excellent, I assure you.'

Richenda resisted the temptation to help herself, and refused with distant politeness, taking instead a piece of cheese from the plate set near her other neighbour. Their host's courtesy had not extended to an introduction, so she did not know his name, but he was the man she had seen from the walls, clearly a superior officer – second in command, she supposed.

He was almost as fair as herself, tall, slender and graceful, with lazy light eyes and a look of indolent good humour. Now he smiled at her.

'You are not without courage, Mistress

Farrell,' he said in a light, amused tone. 'I would not have taken such a risk.'

'But then you,' she pointed out, 'are not in my position.'

'Even less would I in your position.' He leant forward suddenly, his elbows on the table, reaching across her for the plovers' eggs and saying softly, 'My lord has a harsh temper, Mistress Farrell, and a way of avenging insults with ... unforgettable effectiveness. Have a care, if you are wise.'

'I do not think there is anything worse which could happen to us,' she returned, then she smiled. 'But thank you for the warning.'

He waved a white hand to dismiss her need for gratitude.

'Never let it be said that Sir Rowland Laverick declined an opportunity to assist a lady.' He gave a rakish twist to his golden moustache, and she laughed. Suddenly her heart was lightened by this unexpected friendliness. It seemed so long since she had been even mildly amused.

She forgot her fear, her wish for revenge, the need for dignity, the unpleasantness of her position, and allowed him to engage her in conversation: light, frivolous, charming conversation, which for that little time helped her to forget all that had happened. She felt almost as if he had brought a little of the distant and entirely unfamiliar world of the court to Black Castle.

He had indeed been at Court, he told her, when they had talked long enough for confidences: like his father before him, his every wish had been to serve the King. It was as regrettable to him as to all honest Englishmen that the Royal service had demanded that every courtier should don sword and breastplate and go to defend his King's honour in the field. Even more regrettable that he should play any part at all in bringing unhappiness to a young lady whose beauty would certainly eclipse that of any fair flower of the court.

'I have ever been moved too easily by the tears of the weaker sex,' he said, with that cheerfully mocking note which asked her not to take him too seriously. 'Unlike our hard young Colonel there, who has no time for such unmanly softness.'

She glanced round at the 'hard young Colonel' and found that he was watching her steadily through narrowed eyes. She sensed that he had in fact been observing her for some time. His expression was unreadable, but a faint contemptuousness crossed it as she turned, almost as if he despised her for so readily abandoning her cool dignity.

Richenda shrugged to show him that she did not care and returned to her neighbour. But that trivial incident had broken the spell and she could not retrieve the cheerful mood of before. Sir Rowland seemed equally to have lost the thread of his entertaining fluency, and Richenda was constantly aware of that hated presence at her other side, for all that she could no longer see him. She knew that he was observing her still.

How the meal would have ended had it not been interrupted, they were never to know. There was a sudden movement, a whispered discussion at the side door closest to the high table. Heads turned to see what had caused the disturbance, and a man broke away from the group and came quickly – almost running – to Lord Devenish. He was travel-stained, unshaven, troubled: his presence proclaimed bad news as surely as if he had shouted it, and a sudden hush fell over the room.

Lord Devenish leaned towards the man and spoke in an undertone and there was a hurried discussion. Watching him, Richenda saw their enemy's face change, darken, his brows drawn together in a frown: he gave a half-suppressed exclamation, then pushed back his chair with a hasty 'I beg your pardon, ladies', and hurried the man from the hall.

A speculative chatter broke out at once. Even Sir Rowland's cheerfulness had given place to a look of anxiety. He said, rather obviously Richenda thought: 'Bad news, I should guess.'

She was tempted to retort that for her it might on the contrary be very good news; but she took pity on his obvious distress and remained tactfully silent. After all, he had not wronged them as Lord Devenish had done: merely carried out his duty, as he saw it, like any loyal courtier. Parliamentarian though she was, she could not expect a man who had broken the King's bread at court to bear arms against him afterwards.

All pretence of eating was abandoned while the sound of endless inconclusive discussion rose and fell. Jane leaned towards her and whispered, 'Richenda, what do you think has happened? Do you think we should leave the room?'

'I don't know – no, for the moment let's stay. I'd like to find out what it's all about.'

But when Lord Devenish returned at last he was clearly in an uncommunicative mood. He did not look as if he had ever smiled, so grim and lined was his expression, so bleak his eyes. He said only, 'You may retire now, ladies,' and took their hands to escort them to the foot of the stairs.

The dignified course would have been to have left quietly, with due solemnity. But Richenda's curiosity was too much for her. As he released her hand she turned to him.

'May I ask, my lord, whether you have had news of interest to us?'

For an instant the answering light in his eyes frightened her, such an intensity of anger was there in it. He said only: 'Goodnight, ladies,' in a curt tone which was barely polite, and turned away from them.

'You shouldn't have spoken,' Jane reproached her as they reached the gallery and paused to look back at the assembly.

'Why not? I wanted to know.'

Lord Devenish had reached the high table and was leaning across it, gesturing expressively as he talked to Sir Rowland Laverick. The other man was listening with an appalled attention which was marked on every other white and strained face about that table. The ladies could almost see the whispered news passing from the edge of the little group out and down the hall, spreading from man to man like a contagion until it reached the humble seats where the campfollowers waited.

Jane and Richenda stood watching for a long time unobserved, every sense stretched to learn something of what was said. But the elusive news evaded them as it was discussed, passed around, bemoaned below, but never quite loudly enough for them to hear.

It was not until a soldier, despatched to take up his position outside their doors, came running up the stairs, that they were discovered and reluctantly turned to go with him.

'What's happened?' Richenda asked him.

'A battle,' he said non – committally, without looking at her. 'Leicester way, they say.'

'You mean you have suffered a crushing defeat?' Richenda could not quite keep the satisfaction from her tone.

'All is not lost,' returned the man, in a voice which clearly proclaimed the opposite.

In the end, under their persistent questioning, he told them all he knew: how almost the entire forces of the King had suffered a crushing defeat some days ago near a place called Naseby, and now only the west remained in Royalist hands. The man repeated his view – as if trying to convince himself – that the ultimate victory had not yet slipped from their grasp: but when he left them Jane and Richenda were jubilant.

'William will come!' Jane asserted, with shining eyes.

And Richenda had to agree that it was at the least a distinct possibility.

CHAPTER SEVEN

But it seemed that for the time being at least William had more pressing matters to attend to than the rescue of his wife and sister, his home and children. Or perhaps it was simply that the Parliament had a greater need of the necessary siege artillery than he could lay claim to. Whatever it was, he did not come.

The lives of the captive Farrells fell into an uncomfortable pattern. Prayers in Jane's room, lessons for the children in the morning, sewing and talk in the afternoon until it was time for the ordeal of supper in the Great Hall. They dressed more discreetly after that first day, knowing that they had made their point, though they were careful never to appear untidy or slovenly; and they never again found that huge numbers of soldiers waited to watch their arrival in the hall.

But for all that Richenda never quite lost her fear of that moment when the summons came to eat, her tremor of anxiety as to what they might have to face. Never once did she meet with discourtesy, or any humiliation greater than that of having to eat with their enemy; but she could not shake off the knowledge of what he might do if he chose.

It was horrible, too, for them all to feel strangers in the home they loved, to see their rooms, their belongings, every part of their lives desecrated by their enemies. They saw them lolling at their ease, swearing and drinking and gambling where once William had entertained his friends, or family festivals had been celebrated; to see the kitchens uncared for – one visit to that region was too much for the houseproud Jane. The courtyard was littered with rubbish; even the inner rooms missing the woman's touch, degenerating slowly to total squalor.

For all their freedom to go where they pleased there was nothing they could do about it. There were no servants to command, and under the ribald gaze of the soldiers neither Jane nor Richenda cared to tackle the task themselves.

Worst of all, without doubt, to Richenda at least, was the boredom. No riding – no fresh air even – no walking, nothing to do at all but sit and sew, or talk, or play with the children. Only her thoughts afforded any possible amusement, and even that was limited. It was too painful to think of the past; too frightening to consider the future; and she wanted above all to escape from the present. Which left open only a retreat into fantasy, unpromising and impossible daydreams of mild adventure and excitement, of heroes coming to her rescue.

But however her dreams began, they always seemed to bring her back to one single obsessive point: Lord Devenish, and how she hated him. As Daniel Bridge, whatever his shortcomings of courtesy and pride and temper, she had found cause to thank him, reason enough – if only in his appearance and his strength – to turn him into an adequate hero. But he had betrayed her in her dreams as in life, brought them to this, proved beyond all doubt that he was as utterly, irredeemably evil as the rumours said of him.

Richenda had never hated easily, never even, in all her life, hated anyone before, as far as she could remember; but she hated him with a complete and overwhelming intensity, hated his biting tongue and sharp temper, his acceptance of cruelty, his enjoyment of their plight, his treachery. Most of all the fact that she could not look at him without that uncomfortable, disturbing inner tremor made her hate him as she could never have hated any other human creature. She felt almost that if the opportunity lay within her power she would like to kill him, slowly, with her own hands.

She was thankful, at least, that they saw little of him, even at supper.

They had suffered five days of this irksome captivity when he made an unexpected return to their attention. He had been absent from supper that day, and the meal had been the more agreeable as a consequence. Generally after that first day Jane and Richenda sat together at the end of the table, which was less obtrusive and more companionable: always Sir Rowland Laverick joined them, with his easy charm and elegant conversation. Once they were reassured that nothing unpleasant awaited them, the meals became almost enjoyable, a more interesting interlude in an otherwise tedious day.

But today the lighter mood evaporated the moment they reached the foot of the stairs which led from their own floor to that of the children above. Nurse came hurrying down to meet them, her face white with dismay.

'Oh, Dame Farrell, it's Mistress Elizabeth–!' she burst out.

'Why? What's wrong?' Jane's voice was sharp with anxiety. 'Is she sick? Has she had another nightmare?'

The only visible ill-effect of Elizabeth's ordeal in the garden the other day, apart from an increase in her natural reserve, was a recurring nightmare, which seemed to afflict her at the same time each evening. But this time the trouble was not so simple.

'No, madam– Oh, how I wish it was! No, she's gone, madam, disappeared.'

'Gone? But how? Where? What happened?'

'I wish I knew, madam.' Nurse was becoming tearful. 'One moment she was asleep, then I must have nodded off for a minute myself. The next thing she was gone, gone without a trace, and I don't know where! Oh, madam, I've hunted high and low as far as it's safe, but I can't find her – and I daresn't leave the little boys for long, for fear ... for fear the same happens to them.'

'Then we'll search,' broke in Richenda. 'Jane, come with me – she must be somewhere, surely. Perhaps she wanted to explore.'

Jane shook her head.

'No, she was too frightened. She would never have wandered alone ... oh, what's become of her?'

A deep voice broke in. 'Dry your eyes, madam, all is well.'

They turned, sharply. Behind them stood Lord Devenish smiling slightly, and in his arms he carried Elizabeth, eyes closed, limp and motionless.

Jane gave a cry and ran forward.

'Steady now, or you'll wake her. She's asleep.'

Nurse and Jane together seized the child, Jane sobbing with relief.

'What happened? What did you do with her?' asked Richenda sharply.

'She was merely sleep-walking, Mistress Farrell,' he returned coldly. 'I found her crossing the great courtyard.'

Jane turned.

'Sleep-walking?' She pressed a hand to her cheek. 'Dear heavens!'

'It's not unusual,' said Lord Devenish. 'I believe I did the same myself as a child, from time to time.'

'Is that supposed to be reassuring?' demanded Richenda. 'Are we to thank heaven for the remote possibility that she might grow up like you?'

'You can do as you please,' he said curtly. 'But I suggest the child's door is locked at night, for her own safety.'

'Poor little lambkin,' murmured Nurse, sitting on the stair and cradling the child in her arms. 'It's no wonder she's troubled, after all that's come to her. Everything upset

– and that nasty time in the garden. It's my view she should have been taken to play down there afterwards, once or twice, to try and forget it all – but the poor little mites have not had one minute in the sunshine since that day – may God forgive you all, for I won't, that's for sure!' She ended with a scowl at Lord Devenish.

'If that's all that's needed, then take her to the garden by all means,' he returned peaceably. 'I can put a man to keep watch – use it when you like. Just make sure I don't have to turn nursemaid again – I've enough to do without that.'

'No, it must hurt to act so out of character,' Richenda sneered. 'Terrifying children is more in your line.'

'Richenda, why must you speak so?' Jane exclaimed in shocked tones, when he had bidden them an angry goodnight and gone. 'He won't go on taking it so quietly, I'm sure. You'll get us all into trouble.'

'Yes, I suppose so. I'm sorry. It's just that he has such power over us, and he delights in it so – and I cannot bear it that he should be so calm and insolent and have everything his way. I hate him!'

'I know, dear,' said Jane soothingly. 'So do I. But we must keep it to ourselves, it's safer that way.'

After that, at least, they could extend their activities to an occasional excursion. to the garden. The children played more contentedly, and slept more soundly; even the adults felt better for the air and exercise, and learned to endure the inevitable company of the guard at the garden postern.

His was not the only unwelcome presence she must face, Richenda reflected as she came one day in search of the children. Nurse sat dozing in the sun beneath the flowering honeysuckle, and not far away on a low stone wall sat Lord Devenish, cleaning his carbine.

Sharply, the recollection came to her of that other time when she had found him here intent upon his work, in such very different circumstances; but that was over now, and she knew what kind of man he was, and took no pleasure in the memory. At least this time they were not alone. Elizabeth watched him a little uncertainly from a distance; but Jeremy shared his seat and leaned eagerly over, asking questions; and he was receiving, Richenda noted, comprehensive explanations, patiently given.

Lord Devenish looked up as she approached, and his mouth hardened into a thin line.

'Your aunt Richenda is not best pleased,' he remarked caustically to Jeremy.

'I thought at least you'd have the decency to let us enjoy the garden in peace!' Richenda exclaimed, forgetting all her promises of restraint.

'Ah, but as you have been quick to observe, decency is not my strong point, Mistress Farrell. Besides, I came here first. Be thankful at least that I did not turn the children away for disturbing me.'

'I wish you had done so. They should not have stayed, finding you here.'

'Oh dear,' said Nurse, stirring out of her sleep. 'Dame Farrell said nothing of it – I didn't know.'

'I wanted to stay,' broke in Jeremy. 'I like him better than when he was Daniel Bridge.'

Knowing Jeremy's fear of hawks, Richenda was not impressed by this testimonial. 'You must not talk to him, Jeremy. He's a bad man.'

Elizabeth returned quickly to sit beside Nurse. Jeremy stayed where he was, but looked a little unsure of himself.

'A loyal child,' observed Lord Devenish flippantly.

'Why are you trying to insinuate yourself with them?' demanded Richenda. 'Can't you let them alone?'

'I see: you want me to be unpleasant. Blows and angry words – a quick display of temper. Is that it?'

'It would be more in character,' she retorted.

His eyes flashed.

'You see,' he went on confidingly to Jeremy, who began to grow progressively more uncomfortable, 'your Aunt Richenda only likes smooth tongued gentlemen – like our friend Laverick of the honeyed words and neatly-turned compliment.'

'At least *he* doesn't delight in the sufferings of others. You do not realise, perhaps, that I saw what happened when your men sacked the castle – you know at least what I went through.'

'You seem to forget that Laverick played no small part in the taking of the castle, Mistress Farrell.'

'But he did not plan it or command it. He was not responsible for letting the men wreak what havoc they would. He did not win his way into our confidence only to betray us.'

'This is not a court masque, Mistress Farrell: we are at war. Or had you forgotten?'

'That does not excuse cruelty and treachery and brutality. My brother William is a soldier, but I know that no prisoner of his is ever ill-used, no woman or child maltreated.'

'Nor, may I remind you, have you suffered harm at my hands – though one would not think it to hear you.'

'That is only because it serves your purpose to keep us safe. You were not so considerate to those other poor souls.'

'But then do we not all act from self-interest, Mistress Farrell, when it comes to the point?' he returned cynically. 'Even your precious William only behaves as he does because he would not sleep easy at nights if he did otherwise. Let him harden himself, or find a good sleeping draught, and he would have no more scruples than I.'

She gazed at him with contempt.

'How typical, that you should not even be able to recognise common humanity when you see it! How anyone could hope that the King's cause would prosper when such as you uphold it, I can't imagine. Come, Jeremy, and you, Elizabeth. Nurse and I will take you indoors. The air is purer there.'

She heard him laugh as they walked away.

The captives became aware, over the next few days, of a subtle change in the atmosphere, a new sense of urgency and activity. They saw no particular significance in it, until one morning Richenda and Jane looked from the window of the gallery on to the great courtyard, and saw that once again the sheep had been driven into that confined space. They found a stray soldier and demanded an explanation. Were they,

Jane asked eagerly, expecting another siege?

'Why no,' said the man with surprise, as if the very idea was beyond understanding. 'They're to be driven to Bristol.'

'To Bristol!' exclaimed Jane. 'But why?'

'Why do you think?' returned the man impatiently. 'Even soldiers have to eat.'

'William's sheep to feed Royalist soldiers? Never!' said Richenda. 'I am going to see Lord Devenish.'

'No!' Jane clutched at her, but Richenda shook her off. Her indignation carried her at speed along the passages, past curiously glancing soldiers, to the steward's room above the gatehouse where their enemy had installed himself.

She had almost reached the door when it opened, and Lord Devenish came out; saw her, and paused, closing the door. He stood gazing at her in silent astonishment for a moment or two: she could not read his expression in the dim light of the narrow passage.

'Well, well,' he said at last, 'I should indeed consider myself honoured. To what do I owe this visitation?'

Richenda wasted no time.

'Is it true that you're driving the sheep to Bristol?' she demanded.

'Myself and a number of others, yes. Prince Rupert is strengthening the garrison there. Food is—'

'How dare you!' she interrupted furiously. 'How dare you rob William of his beasts to feed his enemies! You have no right to do it!'

'I have every right as conqueror of this castle to do what I please with it and everything within it!' She knew this time that he was in an uncontrollable rage, that she had goaded him at last beyond the limits. 'You do not seem to accept for one moment that you are defeated and at my mercy. You have no rights, no possessions, no life even if I do not choose. Yet you have nagged at me daily like a scolding henwife as if nothing had changed and I was still a despised servant within your gates. God, if you were my sister I'd have beaten you into submission long since! No wonder you're not wed yet – no man would knowingly take such a shrew to wife. You taunt me, insult me, and upbraid me with my harsh treatment – any other man would have done what I should have done right at the start – raped you and hanged you from the nearest tree!'

'Any other man wouldn't think a woman worthy of protection only if he could use her to shelter behind!' Richenda felt the sharp blow of his hand strike her face, and gasped.

'How dare you! How dare you!'

'I'll do worse soon if you don't get out of my sight!'

She glared at him, her palm to her stinging cheek, and turned to go. She was too furious still to feel defeated.

At the corner she felt his hand grasp her shoulder.

'I thought I told you not to walk unattended?' he demanded.

'I'm not afraid of you. You've no woman to hide behind here!'

'Then, by God, you should be!'

In a moment he had swung her against the wall, his hands penning her in; and before she could protest he had silenced her with the full force of his mouth upon hers. She struggled wildly, tried to cry out, hammered her fists against his back. But inexorably his arms drew her to him, held her mercilessly in their strong grasp, so that she was acutely aware of every hard angle of his muscular body.

Then, suddenly, she did not want to struggle any more. His hold did not slacken, but his hands slid down her back, caressing, seeking the slender curves of her slight form, and at every touch the power to resist melted swiftly out of her. If his arms had not been about her she would have slid to the floor, so helpless were her limbs.

The harshness of his mouth on hers lessened, his lips moved, found her throat, and she tilted back her head and closed her eyes and cried out with delight and longing for him to go on, to take her, here, at this very moment.

It was then, when she could no longer bear it that he should release her, that he did so, suddenly and without warning. She sank back against the wall, breathless, dazed, not understanding what had happened to her. Lord Devenish stood watching her, breathing hard, his face dark and stormy.

'Now you know,' he said harshly. 'Keep out of my way in future!'

And he left her.

Richenda ran trembling and sobbing to her room, and threw herself on the bed, her fists drumming furiously on the pillow.

'I hate him! I hate him! May God damn him to hell – and soon!'

It was not difficult for Richenda to avoid Lord Devenish after that final humiliation, for she heard next morning that he had ridden out at dawn with the flock of sheep and twelve men. She told Jane, with emphasis, that she was delighted he had gone; and Jane agreed wholeheartedly.

But, oddly, life was curiously flat without him. His going had left an empty space where her hatred had been, a lack of excitement. Even Sir Rowland Laverick, left in charge, seemed less delightful a companion without the contrast of his commanding officer's churlish manner.

Still, the tension did relax, though they did not find themselves any more free for the change. They knew now that there was nothing to fear at supper time: Sir Rowland was the perfect host, unfailingly charming, attentive, mindful of their needs. He sought them out at other times, too, offering himself as escort to Richenda when Jane was too tired to go out, helping the hours to pass more easily and agreeably – not only because he was good company, but because she felt flattered to think a man so experienced in the ways of the world should find her worthy of attention.

The days passed, then the weeks. June was over, July was going fast. On hot days they sought the shady areas of the garden, or sat inside with every door thrown open; when it was cooler they sat about the fire in Jane's room, and tried to fill the hours as best they could. It seemed hard to believe that they had ever known a different, fuller life: that they had ridden over the hills, or visited neighbours; hunted, or eaten their meals beneath the trees by a little stream; rejoiced at the bringing in of the harvest, worshipped at the little church in the village. Or even that they had spent their days busy with the household tasks and the supervision of servants. That old life seemed no more substantial than a dream.

July was turning to August one hot morning when Jane woke with a headache, and Sir Rowland led Richenda to walk in the garden while the children studied their lessons under Nurse's inexpert eye. The air was still and heavy and scented with late roses, and the war seemed very far away. They had long since ceased to notice the presence of the guard.

From where she walked with Sir Rowland, Richenda could not see him in any case; the apple trees, heavy with ripening fruit, shielded him from sight. That this was no accident, but a deliberate ruse on Sir Rowland's part she did not recognise at first; not, that is, until he paused suddenly in his unhurried progress, and turned to take her hand in both his.

'Mistress Farrell, fairest of mortals—'

Richenda's eyes widened in astonishment, but there was a certain exhilaration in being addressed as the 'fairest of mortals', so she said nothing. Sir Rowland caressed her hand and raised it lovingly to his lips: the kiss he placed upon it was soft and lingering.

'One insufficient token of my adoration, Mistress Farrell,' he explained, transferring her hand to his breast and holding it there. His blue eyes gazed languidly into hers. 'Might I – dare I indeed? – press upon those sweet rosebud lips another, dearer token of the emotion which beats – feel it, Mistress Farrell – beats, as I say, within this doting breast?'

For a brief instant Richenda felt an alarming urge to giggle. Then unbidden into her mind came the recollection of that other kiss, unasked for, unwanted, brutally given, of the caressing hands, the feel of that powerful body against hers through the light fabric of her gown. Suddenly she had no patience with Sir Rowland's perfumed phrases, with his delicate compliments and courtier's gestures.

They were all the same anyway, these men, she told herself, wanting only one thing, however they set about it. She withdrew her hand sharply, leaving Sir Rowland looking a little foolish with his empty hands clasped to his 'doting breast'.

'When all is said and done, sir,' she said haughtily, 'we are at war, and you are my enemy. While that is so there can be no more than civility between us.'

She saw that she had angered him, as far as it was in him to be angered. She had never seen him so much in earnest before as with that naked flash of ill humour in his eyes. But it did not linger for long, and gave way instead to his customary indolent equability of temper.

'So be it, mistress,' he agreed, a little ruefully, and offered her his arm, ready to walk on. He did not refer to the incident again, and it might never have happened for all the difference it made. It changed nothing between them.

And then Lord Devenish returned. Or so they heard from a talkative soldier posted at their door: he came after supper, just before dark, and he was to leave again in the morning – this time, as the gathering of beasts in the courtyard told them, he was taking the cattle to Bristol. They were not likely to see him while he was here.

'Thank goodness for that!' said Richenda, pacing the room, and wondering whether to risk a walk about the castle. Discretion won when she remembered what had happened before, and she stayed where she was; but to their consternation Lord Devenish paid them a brisk visit, unannounced, just as they were about to go to bed.

Richenda felt the colour rush to her face and sank down weakly on the window seat, her heart beating fast. As if from a great distance, she heard Jane greeting him with calm good manners.

'I leave again in the morning,' he was explaining in return. 'I thought it best to see if you had any complaints or anxieties before I left.'

Richenda took a deep breath, and brought herself under control. 'Only that we are still your prisoners, and that you have not yet suffered the fate you deserve,' she said acidly.

He turned to her and bowed, his eyes mocking.

'That you are unchanged, Mistress Farrell, is hearteningly clear.'

'I see you are making a new career for yourself,' she went on, ignoring Jane's reproving glances. 'First a shepherd, now a cowherd! Very useful if you wish to take another castle. Alternatively, it should stand you in good stead when the war is over and you are defeated and need to earn your living.'

His eyes narrowed. 'Do you want me to teach you another lesson?' he asked.

Jane looked up curiously, wondering what lay behind the question. Richenda had kept that particular shameful incident to herself.

'That would please you, wouldn't it?' Richenda snapped back. 'It's just the sort of thing you really enjoy.'

He laughed unpleasantly.

'You may be a spoilt sour-tongued bitch, sweetheart, but you're damned attractive with it,' he said, and left the room. It was clear that the remark was not intended as a compliment.

'What was all that about?' Jane asked. 'Did something happen that I didn't know about?'

Richenda shrugged. 'Nothing of importance,' she said. Then suddenly and inexplicably she burst into tears.

Jane held her, clicking her tongue soothingly.

'Come now, Richenda, what is it, love?'

'I am just so *tired* of all this!' Richenda exclaimed through her sobs. 'I want to go out, and be free and enjoy life again!'

'I know, dear, I know. But we must be brave and patient. William will come, I know he will – you have said so yourself. And one day the war must end.'

Richenda had a sudden bleak vision of years of quiet respectability stretching ahead, tedious, unexciting, orderly. With a new insight she realised that the end of their captivity could not bring her what she wanted from life, nor even could the end of the war. And the worst thing of all was that she did not really know what she was seeking, or what she lacked: only that there was little likelihood that she would ever find it.

But, as Jane said, they must be brave and they must be patient. There was nothing else to do. The unchanging routine was resumed, the only approach to excitement the walks with Sir Rowland, the pleasant mealtimes: if Richenda sometimes felt like screaming or breaking something, she kept it to herself and was outwardly cheerful and good-mannered.

It was only gradually, towards the end of August, that they began to notice a change. At first they were aware only of a greater conviviality at the supper table; and that sometimes the camp-followers, excluded after that first day, were present in the hall, behaving with a freedom which Jane found a little shocking.

Then one day Richenda noticed that Sir Rowland, usually so considerate, was drinking far more than was his custom – that he was in fact rapidly becoming very drunk indeed. He lolled in his chair, rested his booted feet upon the table, laid a caressing hand on Richenda's arm. Jane began to look frightened: Richenda sat very upright, her face an unaccustomed mask of disapproval.

'We have sat long enough at table, sir,' she said. 'You must allow us to leave.'

Sir Rowland lurched towards her and slid a heavy arm about her shoulder.

'Why shweeting, what'sh wrong, then?' he demanded.

'You are drunk!' she said unequivocally.

'Why shouldn't I drink, then?' he asked, with a sweeping gesture. Then he put a hand beneath her chin and tried to turn her head to look at him. 'A man musht have hish pleasuresh, mushn't he?'

Richenda clenched her teeth and gazed resolutely ahead of her.

'Not at the expense of others,' she said. 'You would not behave so if Lord Devenish were here.'

To her relief he released her chin, the easier to lean back his head and laugh, wagging one finger at her.

'How right you are, wench – how right! But hish lordship'sh shafely shut up in Brishtol and can't trouble ush here, ishn't that sho?'

Richenda did turn then.

'What do you mean, shut up?' she asked sharply.

'Bristol is under siege,' explained a more

sober man nearby. 'Since a few days ago. Lord Devenish did not leave in time.'

Richenda swallowed. 'Oh. I see.' She looked round at the increasingly riotous company, and took the law into her own hands. 'Come, Jane, let's leave them to their squalor.'

Sir Rowland reached after her, but he was too drunk for speed. He stumbled, knocked over his chair, and lurched against the table. Jane and Richenda abandoned all dignity and ran.

'I shall never, never eat in that company again!' said Jane with feeling when they reached the safety of her room.

'Nor shall I,' Richenda agreed firmly.

True to her decision, the next time they were summoned to supper Richenda faced the man and expressed her defiance.

'Tell Sir Rowland Laverick that we do not wish to eat with him: we would sooner starve than share his table.'

Looking a little apprehensive, the man set off with his message; and a little later Sir Rowland himself appeared at the door, still relatively sober.

'Did you mistake my meaning, Mistress Farrell?' he asked, with a trace of impatience. 'I bade you both come to supper.'

'Then you can whistle for us,' said Richenda. 'We shall not come to be insulted by you again, as we were last night.'

He looked her up and down.

'There's more of the stiff-necked Puritan about you than I thought,' he said disparagingly, and then shrugged. 'Suit yourselves. I'll send your supper to you.'

It did not make life more exciting to eat in the seclusion of Jane's room, but at least they were not subjected to humiliation and insult. That matters would not improve became quickly evident. The drinking grew deeper, and more prolonged, and soldiers they met about the castle were often drunk and disorderly even early in the day. Mealtimes were extended, beginning sooner, ending late at night, when all those present had drunk themselves into insensibility. Not only that, but Sir Rowland and his companions brought in willing girls from the countryside around, to share their roistering and satisfy their pleasures.

'I did not think our position could be worse than it was,' Jane remarked disapprovingly, as a distant burst of laughter broke in one day on their afternoon quiet. 'But it is. One has to be sure and lock the door, day and night, for one's own safety: and one cannot walk about even accompanied for fear of some insult.'

'Yes,' Richenda said abstractedly. Her hands rested motionless on her lap.

'What are you thinking?' asked Jane.

'I was wondering,' replied Richenda, 'how good their defences are now.'

Jane looked puzzled.

'What do you mean?'

'Lord Devenish said he placed a double guard everywhere, so there was no hope of escape. But whatever Sir Rowland may intend to do, I cannot imagine he's in a fit state, most of the time, to make sure his instructions are carried out – if he's even fit to give any instructions, that is.'

'Yes...' Jane replied slowly, understanding her, a new hope lighting her eyes. 'You mean we might be able to escape? Oh, Richenda, if only–!'

'Steady, though. It wouldn't be easy. Whatever we do we have to make our way through all those drunken brutes to get out: perhaps that's the most dangerous part, I don't know. Also, there are still those who are not always drunk: it's not, I suppose, a vice that appeals to everyone. What we must do, I think, is to keep our eyes open for any unexpected opportunity.'

But none arose. Either the drunken soldiers formed an unpredictable barrier to any escape, or they found that the guards at least were sober and efficient.

Then one morning a minor squabble arose about the date; they realised that it was already well into September; and Jeremy began to complain vociferously that it was nearly his birthday, and where was his father?

'Oh, do be quiet, Jeremy!' Jane exclaimed with uncharacteristic impatience, when his complaints had been repeated endlessly for about half an hour.

'Let's go and see your pony,' Richenda suggested cheerfully, hoping to distract him.

It was not entirely effective, for he

grumbled to herself and Nurse all the way to the stable. But once there he cheered up, and ran to caress the brown pony, who snorted and stretched out a soft warm nose to greet him.

Richenda watched him for a while, smiling, and then went to offer some attention to Bluebell: fortunately the horses had been well cared for, fed and exercised. It was on her way to Bluebell's stall that something else caught her attention. She exclaimed and looked about her, walked quickly around the yard and then returned to Nurse.

'What's up, Mistress Richenda?' asked the old woman.

'There's no one here,' whispered Richenda, her eyes bright with excitement. 'No one at all.'

Nurse glanced round.

'No, mistress. But what of...?'

'No one at the gate there–' Richenda indicated the postern, the one which Dick Price had so fatally guarded that dreadful night. But Dick Price had ridden out with Lord Devenish, and there was no one just now to take his place. 'Nurse, would you be afraid to wait here with Jeremy? Just until I come back.'

'Yes, Mistress Richenda. But–'

Richenda put a finger to her lips.

'Ssh! Stay with the ponies.'

She turned and ran up the stairs, along the passages. An unguarded door, a deserted stable yard – it was too good to be true! If only the others could reach it in time, if only there were no guard the other side! No harm – except in disappointment – if they were discovered in the stables: it would be an innocent enough expedition, easily explained. But once they were through the postern – if they ever went so far – it would be too late for any excuse. And Sir Rowland drunk was a different man from the courteous gentleman of before, unpredictable. They might find they had worse to face than they could have imagined possible. But there was no time to wonder if it was all worth while, no time to consider the risk.

Richenda burst in on Jane and the children.

'Jane, come quickly,' she whispered

urgently. 'Bring the children to the stables – ask no questions.' She did not want to delay matters now with an explanation.

Just as they were, without cloaks or baggage, their only encumbrance Elizabeth's doll, they walked quickly down to the stables. By some miracle they met no one, and arrived to find Nurse and Jeremy still the only occupants of the sunlit yard.

'No guard!' whispered Jane, white-faced, as her eyes fell on the postern.

'You watch the stairs, Jane,' Richenda commanded softly. 'And, Nurse, you keep your eye on the courtyard. And, children, be very, very quiet!'

She was prepared to face stiff bolts, a heavy bar to raise, remembering that other nightmare morning. But to her astonishment the door was unsecured. She turned the heavy ring, the latch lifted, and slowly and smoothly the door swung open. Beyond was a narrow path, a grassy slope, the still dark waters of the moat.

'Jane! Nurse!'

They came, bringing the children, walking quickly, then at a run through the gate and out the other side. Richenda pushed the door to and leant against it. Beside her, Jane gave a tiny hysterical laugh.

'I can't believe it! I just can't believe it!'

CHAPTER EIGHT

'Pull yourself together, Jane,' whispered Richenda in her ear. 'There's still the moat to cross.'

Instantly the brightness fell from Jane's face. Too deep to wade, too wide to jump, the moat lay before them. The only way across was by the drawbridge, and that, they knew, was raised, as always when it was not actually in use. What possible hope was there that three women and three little children, none of whom could swim, could cross that water which had kept whole armies at bay? Jane put her hand to her mouth and looked close to tears. Was this where their hopes would end?

'Follow me,' whispered Richenda next. 'And not a word.'

She turned left along the little path which wound its way beneath the walls, westward, leading away in the opposite direction from the gatehouse. The others followed in a depressed silence, glancing hopelessly, now and then, at the impassable water. Under the tower in which they had lived these past months; on below the high wall of the garden; and they halted at last, at Richenda's signal, within sight of the garden postern. Facing the gate, against the far shore of the moat, gently rocked a little boat, the oars neatly at rest along one side, the line mooring it firmly to a convenient post on the bank. Jane gave a muffled exclamation.

'It's no use!' she whispered despairingly. 'We can't reach it.'

'Ssh!' hissed Richenda. 'Let me think.'

She had known there must be some way across the moat, for the drawbridge was only lowered when a large party had to cross: at other times the soldiers used the posterns for access to the outside world. Which had told her there would be a boat somewhere. What she realised now was that the stable gate had been left unbarred because someone, this morning perhaps, had gone out by it, intending to return.

Supposedly, he knew the boat would be waiting at this side of the castle. He had used it to cross the moat and left it there for his return; left it firmly beyond their reach. There was only one possible solution. She began quickly to pull off her gown and shoes and stockings, and then her shift. Watching her, Jane forgot the need for silence.

'Richenda!' she exclaimed in horror, her scandalised gaze on the slight but shapely figure of her sister-in-law. The children began to giggle, until Nurse silenced them.

'There's no other way,' Richenda retorted severely; and flung herself forward across and into the dark water.

It was cold, shockingly cold to her warm skin, and for an instant the suddenness of it drove all thought of what she must do from her head. Only when the water flooded her mouth and nose and eyes, and its cold grasp began to pull her down, did she remember, and lashed out fiercely, wildly with her arms, kicking her feet, in a clumsy attempt to keep herself afloat.

Just long enough she must stay above

water, just long enough to reach the side of the boat. She stretched out, felt for that reassuring wood, but her hand met only water; water that dragged at her, swamped her.

She kicked again furiously, flailing with her arms, and her wrist fell harshly against a hard surface. It hurt, but heedless of anything except the need to reach the boat, she stretched her fingers, found a hold, and clung on. She brought her other arm alongside, pulled herself towards it, and shook the water from her eyes. She had reached the boat.

She thought that the rest would be easy, but it took much longer than she had expected to drag herself out of the water into the wildly rocking boat. Twice she fell back into the moat, and the second time an oar fell with her, striking her painfully on the side of the head before slipping away beyond her grasp. She gritted her teeth and tried again; and this time, panting and struggling, trying to hold the remaining oar and steady the boat at once, she made it at last.

For a moment or two she lay still where she had landed, to let the temporary dizziness pass. Then she told herself there was no time to lose. Shivering now, she made her slow way across the boat and tried to reach the stump to which it was moored. That, too, like so much today, was just out of reach.

She worked the boat closer to the shore and leapt out, praying that her feet would not miss the bank. Then a moment or two to untie the line, and another leap back into the boat: only just in time did she prevent the second oar from following the first.

Richenda had never rowed a boat in her life, even with two oars: with one she found it very difficult. But at least there was no current in the water to pull her off course, and a trial or two, using the oar as a paddle, set her in the right direction. A few firm steady strokes, an amazingly short space of time, and she was drawing triumphantly alongside the waiting party on the bank.

Jeremy began to jump up and down with delight, Nurse reached down to hold the boat, and Jane gathered up her discarded clothes and came to meet her.

'You must put these on,' Jane urged at once; but Richenda laughed.

'First things first – let's get across.'

There was no time to argue. Richenda reached up to help them one by one into the boat. It sank low in the water as they took their seats, swaying dangerously: Elizabeth turned white and clutched at her mother. Then, when all was still again, Richenda took up the oar and guided the boat back across the moat: it required a greater effort this time, with its added burden. But they made it at last, coming with a little bump to rest at the bank. Richenda reached for the rope and jumped out to moor it safely where she had found it.

Jane lifted the children for Richenda to swing them on to the grass, then the two women followed. And then, as Richenda dressed, her teeth chattering, they stood and looked about as if they could not quite believe what had happened.

'If anyone looks out and sees us, we're done for,' observed Richenda. 'We must get out of sight as quickly as we can. Then we can rest and consider what to do next.'

Beyond the fields which lay to the south of the castle was a thickly wooded valley: that was their nearest point of safety. Nurse gathered Robert into her arms – on foot his slow baby steps would hold them up – Richenda and Jane took the hands of the other children in theirs, and they set off at what was not quite a run in the direction of that sheltering mass of trees.

They did not look around them, they did not glance behind or hesitate until they were in the shade of the wood. Only then, once Richenda had turned to make sure that the castle was no longer visible, did they slacken their pace.

It was a long time since any of them had seen further than the garden of the castle: the narrow windows of their rooms had shown little more than the land just outside, the green slopes where sheep and cattle grazed. And now, all at once, they were following a little path through the trees, seeing how small things had changed since that day in early June when the soldiers had ridden over the hill. The fresh brilliance of the early summer foliage had gone long since, the berries were ripening where the milky blossom had hung thick on the hawthorn, the grasses were light and feathered with seed; and in the fields the corn which had escaped the trampling hooves of the troopers' horses had been gathered and stored in the barns against the winter – not much of it at Black Castle, Richenda knew. Weeks of their lives had passed by unheeded, and autumn had come before they had known it was fully summer.

The delight of it all went to their heads like wine. The children ran and laughed and skipped in the dappled sunlight, the adults walked little less joyously. The air was sweet and fragrant, and they had forgotten it could be so good to be outside, and free, and away from hostile eyes. Away from any creature but shy rabbits and small insects and the delightfully singing birds.

They found a sunlit clearing by a stream and sank down on a mossy bank while the children played about them. Jane discarded her shoes with a sigh.

'I've not walked so far for a long time!' she

said with feeling, rubbing her hot and swollen feet.

'There'll be more walking before the day's out,' Richenda reminded her warningly. Jane looked well enough, for all her tired feet, but it had to be remembered that she was in poor health, and unused to exercise: it was another difficulty to be considered.

For Richenda at least was not so overcome by delight at their freedom to forget how very helpless they were, in many ways. She was happy, certainly, out in the woods again after so long, feeling the sun and air on her face. But she enjoyed too the sense of purpose it gave her after the long aimless weeks to be faced with leading the little party to safety.

Even Jane could not entirely forget why they were here.

'When do you think they'll find we're gone?' she asked, in the tone of one who does not consider the matter very urgent.

'At dinner time, certainly,' said Richenda, 'if not before. But if we're lucky it won't be until then. It gives us a good opportunity to be well away from here before they come seeking us.'

Jane smiled happily.

'I don't know where we'd be without you,' she said.

'Not here, perhaps,' admitted Richenda, 'but we can't end our journey here. This is only the beginning.'

Jane nodded, and slowly digested the thought. 'I suppose it is. Where are we going then?'

'To find William,' said Richenda firmly, 'wherever he is.'

Since it was months since they had heard from William, that decision did not help very much. They agreed after a little that, since he had been heard of last somewhere near Oxford, they should make for the eastern roads.

'At least if Lord Devenish comes back on his way from Bristol, we won't bump into him by mistake,' Richenda commented.

But, they agreed, they must avoid any contact with people who, if questioned, might betray them: pass through no village, halt at no farmhouse, take a road across no town. Yet they had come empty-handed, without cloaks or food or money or transport. It was going to be very hard indeed to reach their destination – or even to survive without help from somebody.

That, however, was a reflection which Richenda kept to herself, realising that if it had occurred to Jane or Nurse, which she doubted, it did not seem to worry them. She tried not to consider how much faith they clearly placed in her to bring them to safety: at seventeen that can be a heady sensation, but also an unnerving one. After all, what else could they have done, faced with their increasingly unpleasant circumstances on the one hand, and that unlocked, un-guarded door on the other?

It was clear that they could not linger very long in that pleasant spot. They must walk as far as they could today, before any pursuit was made, if they were to hope for any kind of safety. The children protested at being dragged away; but Jane told them they were going to find father, and they came willingly enough after that.

It did not take long for the early exhilaration of their escape to wear off. It was pleasant under the trees, but on the stony track beyond the sun beat relentlessly down, the children stumbled and Robert had to be carried, which was tiring for Nurse and then for Richenda, who took him later. Elizabeth became white and silent and very slow, and Jeremy began to complain that his legs were tired; and then went on repeating the information as a constant irritating accompaniment to their journey.

He only gave up when distracted by the realisation that he was hungry, a fact which they were allowed no possible opportunity of forgetting.

It was when she saw the grey weariness of Jane's face that Richenda realised they could go no further. They had no idea how far they had come, though they knew by the position of the sun that they were travelling steadily east. The little deep-valleyed hills of the borders were behind them, the land opening out to rolling fertile downland. They found a sheltered wooded hollow, hidden from any roads or from any vantage point on the hills around, and sank thankfully down on the soft damp dead leaves which littered the ground beneath the trees.

'I'm hungry!' was Jeremy's only comment on their arrival.

Richenda silenced him angrily; Jane had enough to trouble her, exhausted as she was, without that. But she knew that the problem did not end simply because it was not mentioned. They were all hungry, very hungry, and they had no food, nor any obvious means of finding any. Something had to be done very soon if they were to be able to move on in the morning.

'I'm just going to look round,' Richenda whispered to Jane, who was too tired to be interested.

It was almost dusk now, the shadows deepening under the trees; but on the hillside where Richenda found herself after a short but breathless climb the red evening sun was still visible. They had deliberately chosen a track which seemed to follow an unpopulated route; but it was imperative now that they found food, and for that one house at least was necessary. After a lifetime of relatively upright behaviour, Richenda knew she was going to turn thief.

She found the house at last, low mellow

stone buildings at the far side of the valley, sheltered by trees, with cattle grazing close by. It looked as if the war had passed it by, tranquil and hidden in this secret spot.

Richenda had to pass her companions on her way to the house: she paused to tell them not to worry if she were gone for a little while. 'I'll bring you some supper,' she said to Jeremy with a laugh.

She kept as far as possible to the shelter of the trees where the shadows hid her, following a twisting path from one side of the valley to the other; then through the woodlands which surrounded the house. It was very dark there now, and she could scarcely see where she was going. Sudden small noises startled her, twigs snapped unexpectedly beneath her feet; branches and brambles caught at her face and her clothes. She began to wonder if she had lost her way, if she were going endlessly in the wrong direction.

And then all at once the trees ceased and she found herself standing gazing at the house across a narrow meadow. A light glowed faintly gold in a window in the black outline across the dewy silver of the grass. She could make out the dark shape of someone moving against the light, back and forth, and back again. She took a few steps away from the trees into the meadow.

Then a dog barked, the noise sharp, sudden, explosive in the quietness.

Richenda froze, listening, hearing the rattle of his chain: he must be tied up by the back door of the house. Whoever was in the house must have heard him too, for the door opened and the light came spilling out on to the stone flags of the yard. Just in time Richenda slipped back into the shadows, and prayed they would not loose the dog on her.

The man came out into the light, and she saw clearly the outline of a weapon in his hand – a carbine, probably. He stood for several minutes, looking about him; and then, the dog having quietened, he went back into the house and closed the door.

What now? Richenda thought. There was no sense in going on: if the dog did not attack her, or she managed to avoid him, his barking would warn the occupant, and she was not willing to risk the gun. Nor was she willing to reveal herself to the man and appeal for his help. She had learned with painful force that trust could so easily be misplaced.

Then she thought of the cows she had seen grazing in front of the house. Milk would be better than nothing and she had, once or twice, for amusement, milked a cow. Only a container was lacking.

She studied the long range of outbuildings extending at a right angle behind the farmhouse: somewhere there she might perhaps find something she could use. Very likely the dog's chain would not reach so far, and there was a chance she might make her way to the shed furthest from the house without being found by its occupant.

She followed the edge of the wood round until she came as close as she could to the buildings, then she darted across to the nearest open doorway she could see. The dog's barking grew frantic and deafening and he leaped and dragged at his chain.

Richenda heard the door open, the man shout: there was no time to waste. She could see nothing in the blackness of the shed, but groped about for anything, whatever it was, which might serve her purpose. She could hear the heavy clatter of the man's boots on the flags as he made his way across the yard.

She had it at last: exactly what was needed, a solid wooden bucket, heavy but empty. She seized it and ran as fast as her legs could carry her into the wood. A shot rang out, but missed her by yards. She sank panting on to the undergrowth and lay still with the blood drumming in her ears. Slowly the dog's barking ceased, and at last she heard the door close.

And she had her container. She felt very weary now, too weary to move: she wished she could stay where she was until morning. But there was no sense in that, and in any case the others were waiting, hungry and anxious, across the valley.

Very slowly she forced her reluctant legs on, through, the trees again – the bucket was a tiresome encumbrance in the enclosing darkness – round the house to the front. No dog barked now, all was quiet but for the gentle sound of the cows munching steadily at the lush grass. They must have been milked that evening, but she found one willing enough to submit to giving up a little more. With satisfaction, Richenda heard the sweet whiteness sing into the pail.

She did not notice much about her return to the others. She was aware only of the need to get there somehow, with the milk still safe in the pail. It was not so easy when roots and brambles lurked to trip the unwary, and her legs were only too ready to give way.

It was completely dark by now, and their faces were only a white blur in the night when she came on them, guided by the faint rustling as they moved.

'Thank goodness you're back,' whispered Jane with an intensity which showed how anxious she had been. 'We heard a shot.'

Elizabeth and Robert were asleep, but not Jeremy. 'What's for supper, Aunt Richenda?' came his voice, clear in the quietness.

'Milk,' said Richenda. 'I found a cow.'

'But I don't like milk!' And he began to howl.

Exasperated beyond endurance, Jane

slapped him. 'It's all we've got, so be thankful!' she said sharply.

There was not a great deal of milk, and Richenda insisted that Jane and the children had most of it: they did not wake Elizabeth and Robert, but left their share for the morning. They were none of them satisfied when they settled down at last to sleep. The ground was damp, they were cold and exhausted and hungry; but if nothing else, at least they were free.

They awoke to a steady drizzle and chilled and aching bones. The prospect drained every last trace of yesterday's light-heartedness out of them. They did not particularly wish to be back at Black Castle, as things were, but they would gladly have been almost anywhere else.

The trees gave as much protection as they could hope for from the rain and it was tempting to linger there. But Richenda feared that the farmer disturbed last night might spread his search further afield and come on their hiding place; and Elizabeth, never very strong, was already developing an ominous cough. The sooner they found William the better.

'Once we're well away from Black Castle we can make some enquiries,' she said to Jane. 'I don't think they'll pursue us very far, and we can't just go on hoping, to come on William by chance.'

So when the milk was drunk they left the pail where its owner might find it and set out, heads bent against the rain, through the valley and over the hill and on, and on, to the east.

Hungry as they were, the children's energy faded very quickly. Richenda took Jeremy and Elizabeth on her back by turns; Nurse plodded on with Robert in her arms, putting him down to walk when she could go no further; Jane looked as grey and weary as she had last night. The morning passed slowly, and about midday the rain ceased: that at least brought some relief, though they were thoroughly drenched by now, shivering in the cold greyness which followed. Their shoes, designed for light indoor wear, were already falling apart, leaving their feet to the mercy of stones and thorns. Even Richenda's boundless optimism began to fade.

What had she done, she wondered, leading her helpless little party so unprepared into so hazardous a journey? However far they walked, what hope had they, if she were honest, of ever finding William, who might by now be in any part of England – or Wales, or Scotland, or even perhaps Ireland? she reflected dismally. They would be fortunate, rather, to survive another day or two. Better far the mercies of Sir Rowland Laverick than this!

Early in the afternoon, as far as she could tell, their track led through a beech wood, the way edged with bracken and high mossy banks. It was here that Jane suddenly turned aside with a low moan and sank down in the bracken, her eyes closed and her face ashen. Richenda eased Jeremy from her back and ran to Jane's side.

'Just a little further, Jane,' she urged. 'We'll find the nearest house and ask for help.'

'I can't,' Jane said faintly.

Nurse set Robert down and came to rub Jane's hands. 'She's walked too far already,' was her opinion, and Richenda had to agree.

'If we can carry her up there,' she nodded to the right of the path 'out of sight, you and the children can wait with her and I'll go and find help.'

The children gazed at her mournfully: today Jeremy was too weary to complain. Their eyes seemed full of reproach for Richenda at having brought them to this plight.

'Not much else we can do,' agreed Nurse. 'I'll take a look up there and see where's a good place before we move her.'

She set off through the bracken and up the bank. Then Elizabeth called, 'Aunt Richenda, there's someone coming!'

Her sharp ears had caught the sound first, but now they all heard it: the steady rhythmic thudding of horses' hooves – many horses' hooves – coming this way.

'Quick!' said Richenda to the children. 'All of you, up there – find the best place you can and lie flat on the ground. Come now, Jane dear, put your arm round my neck and I'll help you up there.'

Together she and Nurse half-dragged, half-carried Jane to a mossy ledge above the road and laid her there well out of sight. The children lay, wide-eyed, on their stomachs and listened to the approaching horses.

There were other sounds now, above that of the horses' hooves: the rattle and jingle of harness and the voices of men, singing.

'Soldiers,' whispered Richenda. She crept forward and peered over the ledge on to the track. They were not in sight yet, but the singing came more distinctly now: she could begin to make out the words:

'The strength that doth our foes with-stand,

O Lord, doth come from thee;

Thou art, O God, my help at hand,

A fort and fence to me...'

A psalm, unmistakably a psalm! She had heard of no Royalist troop who would sing psalms as they marched. She turned to the others, her face alight with relief and joy.

'They're ours! Oh, Nurse, they're ours!'

'Don't let them see you until you're sure,' Nurse warned her.

They came into sight at last, riding in

orderly file along the road, breastplates and helmets gleaming in the greyness, orange sashes a bright splash of colour, the rhythmic unison of their singing of a piece with the precision of their progress along the road. Troopers of the New Model Army, exactly as William had described them in one of his letters, the product of the reorganisation set in motion by Parliament in the early spring: the army which at Naseby had justified its existence once and for all.

Richenda jumped up and ran and scrambled her way down the bank to the track, slithering to a halt before the foremost rider. She presented an odd sight, if she had paused to consider the matter. Slim and pretty, but with her lovely hair tangled and lank from its soaking, her green gown torn and mud-stained, her slippers in shreds: as a country girl in homespun she might have looked merely disreputable, but wearing a gown which had once been edged with fine lace and trimmed with satin ribbons she looked very strange indeed.

She had cause, however, to be thankful for

the iron discipline of the Parliamentary troops. The officer gave the word to halt and they halted, neatly and without hesitation: a low whistle, abruptly broken off, was the only tribute any man gave to her appearance.

'Now then, wench,' said the officer, a dependable-looking middle-aged man, 'what can I do for you?'

Richenda had not thought what she should say: there was so much they needed. But one thing above all perhaps they could tell her. She assumed her most haughty bearing to counteract the mud stains.

'I am seeking Sir William Farrell,' she said. 'I wonder if you can give us news of him?'

The man's eyebrows rose.

'Sir William Farrell, eh? And what would you be wanting with him?'

At least the name was not unknown to him. Involuntarily, Richenda smiled, which had a disturbing effect on the officer. As a good Parliamentarian, he suppressed it, and listened attentively to what she had to say.

'He is my brother,' she said. 'His wife is with me, and his children, and their nurse.

We have come from Black Castle to find him.'

'Black Castle! That's a tidy way – and we heard Black Castle was held by Lord Devenish.'

Richenda nodded.

'We escaped,' she said briefly. 'But, sir, we must find my brother soon or we shall die. I beg you to help us.'

The officer glanced up the bank. Two small butter-yellow heads were just visible above the grass, and one brown one; behind them Nurse watched anxiously.

'I'll see what we can do,' he said. 'You get them all down here, mistress.'

The soldiers moved off a little way to where the road widened into a clearing, and halted there. They dismounted, and lit a fire, and by the time Richenda had summoned the weary group there were signs that a meal would soon be ready. Jeremy watched wide-eyed as bread and cheese were set out on the grass, and edged slowly nearer to that enticing point until a soldier turned to him with a smile, and – the greatest wonder of all – broke off some bread for him to eat.

They made Jane comfortable on blankets spread for her, and covered her over.

'Food first,' said the officer practically, 'and then we'll talk.'

If they always had to wait so long between meals, Richenda reflected as they ate, they would never need rich or lavish food again. The simple bread and cheese and stewed rabbit was a banquet to the truly hungry, exquisitely flavoured, everything they could desire. She watched life and colour and cheerfulness return to the faces of the children and Nurse, and at last to Jane, and was profoundly thankful for the chance which had brought the soldiers this way in their moment of greatest need. She felt sure, for the first time since leaving home, that their troubles would soon be over.

When they were satisfied at last the children curled up at their mother's side, and went to sleep; Jane slept too, and Nurse. But Richenda fought her own drowsiness and gave her attention to the next problem.

'Sir William Farrell's only ten miles or so from here,' the officer assured her, to her delight. 'Just this side of Gloucester, at some little place – can't remember the name, but you should find him easily enough. He had a lot of heavy stuff with him, so he's not moving fast. I'd give you an escort so far if I could, but I can't spare anyone just now. Still, you should be safe enough – we hold all this area now, so you'll not meet with any trouble – they'll certainly not ride out from Black Castle to seek you hereabouts. Two miles up the road there's a village with a good inn: I should get yourselves there for the night, and you'll be ready to go on tomorrow – I reckon Dame Farrell's in no state to go much further.'

It sounded ideal, but Richenda gazed at him in silence, reddening with embarrassment. They could not stay at an inn without money, but she could not bring herself to beg.

Nor, as it happened, did she need to. The officer noticed her discomfort, thought for a moment, and then pulled a jingling purse from his pack.

'Just in case you're a bit short,' he remarked casually, as if it had just that minute occurred to him. 'Always comes in handy to have a bit of spare cash.'

Richenda was not so foolish as to refuse, but his kindness overwhelmed her. She could hardly speak for the grateful tears which rose as she thanked him. He patted her on the shoulder.

'Don't mention it, Mistress Farrell. Glad to be of service.'

Soon afterwards, pressed for time, the soldiers left them. Jane woke before they went, and added her thanks to those of Richenda, and heard the good news the soldiers had given her.

'Oh, Richenda,' she exclaimed, 'I am so thankful–!' And then she paused. 'What day is it – the date, I mean?'

'I don't know– Oh yes, it was the thirteenth when we left home – you remember the time we had with Jeremy about it. How many days have gone since then – oh!'

Jane nodded, her eyes bright.

'Yes, tomorrow is Jeremy's birthday: tomorrow, when we shall see William!'

After that it was easy to persuade the

children to walk a little further. Jeremy skipped and sang and would have made the rest of the journey doubly difficult for the weary adults, had he not suddenly realised that his new clothes had been left behind at Black Castle: the fine boy's clothes he should have put on in honour of his birthday. He was not completely cast down, but he walked more calmly after that.

Even so, they were almost ready to face the whole ten miles today. But at that Richenda overruled them. The two miles to the inn would be quite far enough, and it would not do to be too ill from exhaustion to reach William at last. Besides, they might lose their way in the dark.

It was sensible advice, of course, so to the inn they went.

It was low and honey-coloured and welcoming. They were brought warm water for washing, and more food and drink, and promised the use of a horse and cart for their journey tomorrow; and then shown to two rooms where soft and white-linened beds were invitingly ready, and fires burned cheerfully in the hearths. Richenda insisted that Jane went to bed at once.

'You want to look your best tomorrow,' she said.

It was an unanswerable argument.

'I'm so glad it's all over,' said Jane thankfully.

'So am I,' agreed Richenda; but oddly she had to admit to herself that her feelings were not entirely unmixed. She had brought them so far, and tomorrow they would reach the end of their journey exactly as she had hoped; and they would see William, dear William, again after all this time.

'He had a lot of heavy stuff with him,' the officer had said. Thinking about it now, Richenda reflected that he must be on his way to win back Black Castle. It would be fun, she thought, to see the Royalists get their just deserts at William's hands.

But, knowing William as she did, she feared that it would be a pleasure denied to her. William was not one to ask his wife and children, or his sister, to face any further unnecessary danger: and old Aunt Ann Farrell lived at Gloucester, alone in a large house, with ample room for all her relations.

It was more than likely that William would despatch them all there to safety, now that Gloucester was no longer threatened by the Royalists.

Certainly Jane would prefer that, and Nurse. But for herself? The thought filled Richenda with despondency. It would be a tame end to the adventure.

Still, it was foolish to wish for anything else after all they had been through. And even she was glad to feel well fed and warm, and a little cleaner, and to have the prospect of an undisturbed night's rest before her.

She made sure that Nurse and the children were comfortable; and then descended the stairs to make the final arrangements for the morning.

It was in the hall, at the foot of the stairs, that she came face to face with Dick Price.

CHAPTER NINE

It was hard to tell who was the most astonished, Dick or Richenda. Both took a quick indrawn breath, started, and then stood quite still, staring in utter incredulity. The moment of silent amazed recognition seemed to go on and on. And then at last Dick murmured, 'Mistress Richenda!'

It was the first time he had spoken to her since the castle fell by his treachery.

Richenda watched him, thinking through the sudden total confusion of her thoughts. Like them, he was only eight miles away from William, many miles from Black Castle – further still from Bristol, where she had supposed him to be. He had betrayed them, and then joined forces with their enemy, but presumably he had been unable to do anything else, once the castle was theirs. How likely then that he, for so long a loyal and devoted servant, had come to see the full horror of what he had done; turned his back on the man who had led him astray, and come this long way in search of his former master, to earn his forgiveness for his misdeeds. She could see it all clearly, in those few moments; even read it in his face as the colour came and went – shame, embarrassment, hope for the future: she saw them all there. Warmly, generously, putting the past behind her, she smiled.

'You are on your way to William too!' she exclaimed. 'I am so glad! We can go together tomorrow.'

He hesitated for a moment, as a man must who has done a great wrong to the woman who addresses him; and then nervously returned the smile.

'Yes, Mistress Richenda, that's right.' He glanced about him. 'Have you seen the landlord? I need fodder for my horse.' His eyes reached the window, and brightened.

'Ah, there he is! – One moment, Mistress Richenda – I'm too much the good groom to leave a horse untended – I'll be with you in a moment.' He turned to go, and then paused: '"We" did you say? You're not alone then?'

'No. Dame Farrell is with me, and the children, and Nurse. We've had a bad time since we escaped, but it's nearly over. They're sleeping upstairs.'

Dick nodded.

'I see. You've done well to come so far.' He grinned suddenly. 'And here I am gossiping while that poor beast goes hungry. Excuse me, mistress.'

He left her then, and she stood gazing after him, reflecting on the astonishing coincidence of it all. A voice at her elbow broke into the thoughts.

'Can I help you, mistress?'

She turned: the round kindly figure of the landlord stood at her side.

'Oh!' she said, a little surprised. 'Dick thought he'd seen you outside – he's gone to look for you. He wants fodder for his horse.'

The man shook his head.

'Is this Dick one of your party? I thought you all came on foot. I'm a mite short of space in the stables just now–'

'He is an old friend,' she explained. 'He'll be coming with us tomorrow. But we shall still need the cart, if you're able to let us

210

have it. That's–'

Someone came in from the yard: Dick, she supposed, and turned her head to smile at him.

The clear grey eyes she had never thought to see again met her gaze, alight with ironic amusement.

'You're a long way from your nest, my bird,' he said amiably, and bowed with mocking grace. 'Let me have the honour of returning you to it.'

For a dreadful instant, Richenda panicked. She gazed about frantically, as if for some way of escape; ran a little way, and then stopped, remembering with dismay the weary sleeping travellers upstairs. If she ran, would he know about them? Would they be safe?

She saw the landlord's eyes on her, anxious and bewildered. He would help her – but help her to what? And then it was too late. The next moment the hall was full of men, armed and alert. Her arms were held behind her, a pistol levelled at her head, and she watched in helpless dismay as Lord Devenish called four others and ran up the stairs two at a time.

He knew, of course he knew. Dick Price had paused to ask her about the others; and she had told him, told him everything without reserve. For the second time he had betrayed them. Bitterly she remembered her own dictum of yesterday, 'Never trust anyone' – forgotten so soon, and so disastrously.

She heard the children cry out in protest at being wakened, and then in fear; she heard Jane scream. Then she watched as they came slow and stumbling and weeping down the stairs: and she bit her lip to keep back her own harsh angry tears.

Fool that she had been! Stupid blind fool, to trust the man a second time after all that had happened! And they were so near. Eight miles away, maybe less, William would have halted for the night with his orderly disciplined troops. Tomorrow they would have been with him, after facing hunger and cold and weariness to reach the protection of his loving presence.

And because of her moment of carelessness, her discarding of all that hard-learned caution, they had walked right back into the hands of their enemy.

She heard the landlord protesting, good man that he was, but there was nothing he could do against so many. She cried to him 'Let Sir William Farrell know!', with no real hope that word would reach her brother. In any case, what good would that do now?

They were marched out into the yard, where a covered cart, perhaps the one that should have taken them to William, had been hurriedly made ready; and lifted in to sit with the man with the pistol, who watched them relentlessly for any false move. Horses were saddled and mounted, an order called; and slowly, joltingly, the wagon set off, the riders forming an impenetrable escort around it.

So much for her regrets at the end of the adventure! It was almost as if Richenda's silly childish wish had been answered, to show it to her in its true light. Seeing the despair in Jane's eyes, Nurse's grim expression and the too-old grief on Elizabeth's face: hearing Robert crying miserably and Jeremy screaming incessantly

'I want Father! I want Father!', she knew too late what she had wished on them. It was almost more than she could bear.

After a little time the wagon halted and Lord Devenish bent his head under the canopy. 'Be quiet, boy!' he snapped at the still shouting Jeremy. 'You'll see your father soon enough, at home, at Black Castle.'

The words reached Jeremy slowly, and the noise subsided to a sad hiccuping. 'Shall I?' he asked doubtfully.

'Of course,' said Lord Devenish. 'Didn't I tell you so? I'm a man of my word.'

'Of course,' thought Richenda. 'If he's allowed to do so, Jeremy will see his father at Black Castle, aligning his troops to lay siege to the fortress which holds his wife and his children.'

But she had not the heart to explain the cruel subterfuge to the child. Better for him if he took that little comfort for the moment.

It grew slowly darker: the snug firelit bedrooms of the inn seemed very far away from the jolting discomfort of the wagon, as far as their present numb misery was from the peace and safety of this afternoon.

Robert at least was too little troubled by adult anxieties to lie awake for long. He laid his head on his mother's lap, put his thumb in his mouth, and slept. After a little while Jeremy joined him. Elizabeth lay down, clasping her doll for comfort, but her eyes still showed dark in her white face whenever Richenda looked her way.

At last, when it was fully night, the wagon halted. Peering round the broad back of the driver, Richenda could see only that they seemed to be in a wood, dense and with no obvious road through it. That explained the last few dangerously swaying yards of their journey. Around the wagon the soldiers were dismounting, almost without sound. Lord Devenish glanced in at them, and said in a low voice, 'We're halting here for the night. Get what sleep you can: we shall be on our way at dawn.'

There were blankets in the cart, and they huddled beneath them and tried to sleep: there was nothing else to be done. If they had come to this from last night's discomfort they might almost have welcomed it: but having been so very close to their goal, it seemed somehow worse than anything they had yet endured.

The children at least were still sleeping when dawn came. There was no pause for breakfast: each soldier ate his bread and cheese where he stood, even after he had mounted his horse; their own ration was handed to them to be eaten as they travelled. But this time they were none of them very hungry.

No one said anything for a long time, each closed in with her painful thoughts, oblivious to anything beyond. Jane was the first to speak: she said expressionlessly, without real interest, 'He's avoiding the high roads and villages.'

'Of course,' said Richenda. 'He's in enemy country.'

'Perhaps,' Jane suggested in that same apathetic tone, 'if we made a great deal of noise, someone might hear and rescue us.'

'I imagine he'd shoot us first, if he had to.' She glanced at the man with the gun, still sitting with them: Jane followed her gaze.

'Yes,' she agreed, and lapsed once more

into gloomy silence.

The morning passed slowly. The early mist gave way to shafts of hazy sunlight slanting through the trees; the children with the resilience of youth began to chatter among themselves. It was a little while before Jeremy remembered all that had happened, and said with sudden dismay, 'It's my birthday today.'

Then he began to cry, softly and miserably, until Elizabeth said severely, 'He said we'd see Father at Black Castle.'

Jeremy drew his sleeve across his nose – he had long since lost his handkerchief – and subsided into a mute despondency.

Just after midday the furtive cavalcade came to a halt in another wood, in yet another clearing.

'You can get out here,' the man with the pistol – not the same man as last night – instructed them.

They stretched painfully cramped limbs and struggled out into the sunlight, and then stood in a dazed little group looking about them. It was a surprise to Richenda to see that there were only nine men besides

Lord Devenish: in the struggle last night the inn had seemed full of soldiers.

Clearly the halt was designed as much to rest the horses as their riders: no fire was lit to attract attention, and the inevitable bread and cheese, with accompanying ale, was handed to them. They ate and drank standing – unlike the soldiers, who were glad to stretch out on the grass – the children scampering about in the space in the centre of the group.

Across the clearing Richenda could see Lord Devenish deep in conversation with one of the soldiers, gesturing as he talked as if discussing the route. He had neither spoken to them nor even glanced in their direction since they had halted.

Richenda felt a little spark of anger: he had snatched them away at the very moment when they were within reach of their goal; for his own ends, his own protection, he was dragging them back to all they had thought to escape, with scant disregard for their comfort; and now he seemed to have forgotten all about them.

'He does not think of us as people like

himself,' she thought, 'simply as the means to his own selfish ends.' And their usefulness as hostages must be great for him to have ridden out after them at the moment of his return to Black Castle – for so he must have done, she supposed.

She realised in a moment that he was coming their way, and called out, 'I thought you were shut up in Bristol.'

Her tone implied that she greatly wished it were still the case. He turned, and for an instant she was astonished at the change in his expression: sombre, weary, almost haggard – it held no single trace of irony or amusement or even, for the moment, of pride.

'Bristol fell five days ago,' was all he said, curtly.

Richenda's eyes widened.

'Fell? Bristol? But Prince Rupert held it – didn't he?'

'He did,' agreed Lord Devenish, the grim line of his mouth unrelenting.

The invincible Prince Rupert, the King's nephew, who even at Naseby had met with success in his part of the field. And the siege could not have been long, a few weeks merely; and she had heard that Bristol was well-garrisoned and lavishly supplied, the greatest seaport in England, after London.

'What happened?' she asked. 'Did someone betray *you* this time?'

Lord Devenish shrugged, ignoring her shaft.

'He felt the cost was too high in lives lost. That most of all, I think.'

'Then the war must indeed be over,' she said, 'if even he is counting the cost.'

'No war is over, Mistress Farrell,' he reminded her, 'until the final battle is fought and won.' But his eyes were bleak, already defeated.

'So you'll fight your last battle at Black Castle,' she said sharply. 'What use is that?'

'Not much,' he conceded, 'except, I suppose, to me.'

She realised at once that for the first time since she had known him he was talking to her simply, without any barrier of anger or irony or superiority, as one human being to another. It gave her an odd sensation, temporarily shutting out any thought of her present situation, of the wrong he had done her; even, for the moment, of her hate. She found she had been gazing at him for some time, for her eyes met his at last, and then fell at his penetrating glance: she felt the colour rise in her face. Whatever must he have thought?

But Lord Devenish at least had returned to their immediate situation.

'How did you escape?' he asked suddenly. 'I would have thought it impossible.'

'You'll have to ask Sir Rowland Laverick about that,' she returned.

'So you can be sure I shall when we reach Black Castle,' he said grimly, in a manner which made her feel almost sorry for Sir Rowland. Then she realised what his words implied.

'Have you not seen him then?' she asked in surprise. 'I thought you'd come from Black Castle.'

'No,' he said. 'The Bristol garrison was given escort to Oxford: we came from there – by a fortunate route, so it would seem.'

So he had not even been looking for them – did not even know they had escaped! It made their capture so much more bitter, to know that they had so nearly avoided it. If they had spent the night in the woods; or chosen to walk the full ten miles on roads where approaching horsemen were easily seen or heard–!

But they had done neither of those things, and here they were. The brief moment of kindlier feeling towards Lord Devenish had gone. Richenda looked up at him sharply and said:

'Why did you promise Jeremy that he would see his father again? You know as well as I do that if he does it'll be at the other end of a cannon.'

He seemed unable to match her anger.

'What would you have me do?' he asked wearily. 'I had to silence the child – and it's no help to him to be miserable. In any case, it may well be true soon enough. Whatever happens, the war can't last much longer.'

He moved away from her without saying anything more and gave the order to remount.

It began to seem as if they had passed all their lives in the wagon, as the afternoon dragged slowly by. Jolted, cramped, dejected, they endured the journey, knowing that every rut crossed, every pothole avoided, took them surely and steadily another step nearer to the prison they had left. The only comfort Richenda could find in the situation (and it was a very small one) was that at least discipline among the soldiers at the castle would improve with the return of their commanding officer.

She was not sure why she should be so certain of that, after what she had seen on the night the castle fell; but she knew, even from William, that it was a most difficult task to control soldiers in the heat of the attack, and that many officers did not even try. And of the fact that Lord Devenish could control his men if he chose, she had seen ample evidence.

Late in the afternoon one of the soldiers' horses cast a shoe, and while the problem was discussed and the decision made to lead the horse and accommodate the rider on the wagon, Lord Devenish ordered a halt and a rest. 'More bread and cheese,' thought

Richenda ungratefully, as the rations were handed out.

Jane seemed to have lost all hope. Nurse and Richenda half drove her from the wagon, but outside she refused to walk around, only sat in a miserable huddle on the grass gazing into space and saying nothing. Richenda stood anxiously at her side, trying uselessly to draw her into conversation. A little way off Jeremy had struck up a conversation with Lord Devenish.

He had begun by complaining that he should have been breeched today, but had been diverted into more cheerful channels by his companion. Why, thought Richenda, could the child not see, as they all did, what kind of man he was? He was full of some story, eagerly told with energetic gestures and bright eyes: all thought of their plight seemed to have deserted him now. And then Richenda realised what he was saying.

'So,' came his clear young voice, 'Aunt Richenda took all her clothes off and jumped into the moat!'

Lord Devenish made a choking noise in his throat and turned to look at Richenda:

his eyes were dancing. Worse than that, she heard him say enthusiastically to Jeremy, 'I wish I'd been there to see it!'

Furious with Jeremy, thoroughly mortified, Richenda went fierily red and gave as much of her attention as possible to Jane: later, when they were alone again, she would have words with Jeremy!

It was almost time to go. The men were rising reluctantly to their feet, moving to their horses, putting away any items removed from their baggage. And then suddenly one of them, posted some way back to keep watch, rode explosively into the group and cried out in a hoarse whisper, 'There's someone on our tail – no more than a mile back, at most – a troop, maybe more.'

In a matter of seconds they had begun to move: more cramped than ever now in the wagon, with their additional passenger, jolted more roughly with the speed of the journey. But for all the discomfort Jane seemed to have been woken to life.

'William!' she mouthed delightedly to Richenda.

Whoever it was in pursuit, the pace of

their own party was relentless, unsparing; on and on, with no thought of a pause for the night. Darkness fell and the moon rose, and still they went on, an urgent uncomfortable journey through by-roads and lanes scarcely built for a wagon to pass.

And the pursuer did not rest, either, whoever he was. He was further behind once they were on their way, falling back to a safer distance; but always there, never allowing them a moment to pause or hesitate.

At dawn he was still with them, but by now they knew that the country was becoming familiar, with here and there some landmark which they knew: they could not be far from Black Castle. The horses were close to exhaustion, and so were their riders. They could not hope to keep up the unsparing pace of last night.

Now and then the soldiers glimpsed the pursuing troop, and once shots rang out, spurring them on to a sudden burst of speed, soon ended. Inside the wagon the prisoners clung to anything which could give support against being hurtled from side to side, too shaken to speak or think. But through it all Jane's eyes shone with renewed hope. William was there, she knew, and surely, surely he must reach them before they came to Black Castle.

Richenda glimpsed Lord Devenish passing them once, and the tense, grim line of his mouth, the frowning brows, all told her he too knew that they were dangerously hard pressed. She felt a tingle of excitement rise in her, without Jane's hope, but enjoying the chase, the uncertainty, the urgent speed.

And then they came over a hill and Black Castle lay before them, unchanged, tranquil in the midday sun, the moat shining around it clear and unruffled, the drawbridge firmly raised against them.

Lord Devenish despatched a man ahead to give word of their coming: how his horse managed that final extra burst of speed, Richenda did not know, watching the poor foamflecked beast driven on to the water's edge, dragged almost to his knees in the reining in. They could hear their pursuers now, so close were they, gaining on them every moment.

The messenger at the castle was shouting, waving his arms, but the drawbridge did not move: nothing moved, no guard on the battlements, no face at the window. Had no one heard?

They had reached the messenger themselves now, and from the rear of the wagon could clearly see their pursuers, a small swift group of riders coming closer every second, at their head a broad fair man.

'It is William!' shouted Jane in triumph.

And then with a creaking and squealing and an awkward jolting motion the draw-bridge began to move slowly, unsteadily down, inch by slow inch, until it reached the bank in front of them. Just in time, only just in time, for Lord Devenish and his men. Just too soon for their pursuers.

Over the drawbridge they clattered; and as the pursuing horsemen reached it, urging their mounts forward, it began as slowly, as unevenly to move upward, further and further beyond their reach. Jane heard William's great cry of rage and dis-appointment, and fell sobbing on the floor of the wagon. When Richenda turned her head again the gate was down, the drawbridge up.

There was no longer any hope of escape.

CHAPTER TEN

For a few minutes all was commotion in the courtyard of the castle. The soldiers of the garrison scuttled about like disturbed ants, trying to look as if they had been constantly active and alert; Sir Rowland Laverick appeared flushed, unsteady, and filled with consternation, all of which he tried to disguise under an effusively welcoming manner. Their own escort dismounted painfully and led their trembling exhausted horses to the stables.

And through it all Jane sobbed hysterically, uncontrollably, all the tension of the last days giving way to complete despair. The children looked on in frightened sympathy, Robert sobbing too, and Nurse and Richenda tried uselessly to comfort them all.

No one seemed to have any time for them until Lord Devenish, his face a stony mask of severity, came to tell them, curtly, that they could go to their rooms. No concern, no sign that he realised what he had done in dragging them across that drawbridge under William's very nose: Richenda raised her head, her eyes darkened with fury.

'For that piece of cruelty you'll pay dearly, my lord, when William lays his hands on you! Maybe you think to use us as hostages – but make no mistake, however honourable William is he won't let you go free and unpunished for what you have done. I hope they make you die a traitor's death for that – and I'll make sure I'm there to see it!'

She wondered for a moment if he had heard her, so little did his expression, change as she spoke. He only repeated 'Get to your rooms, all of you', and turned away; they had no choice but to do as he said.

He did not even trouble to have them escorted. He had given his attention to Sir Rowland, and they heard him say, with as little warmth as he had used to them, 'Come with me.'

And then they were inside, making their slow way through the great hall, along the gallery and the passages and the winding stairs to those painfully familiar rooms they had left so suddenly and so hopefully just four days ago. Everything was exactly as they had left it, even to Jane's sewing laid hastily aside, and Elizabeth's laboriously worked sampler lying on her little stool.

They got Jane to bed, though she was still beyond any consolation they could offer. Robert at least could find comfort with Nurse, and Jeremy was soon diverted with his favourite toy; but it was Elizabeth now who made Richenda anxious. It had all been too much for her at last, the escape and the pursuit and now her mother's breakdown, and all her long held reserve gave way to helpless tears. Most of all, Richenda found, she wanted the comfort of her doll, her almost inseparable companion, who was, at the moment, nowhere to be found.

Richenda thought desperately. Elizabeth had carried the doll when they left the castle, and had it still when they came to the inn – it hurt her to remember that moment, looking in on the sleeping Elizabeth as she lay at peace in the big bed with her brothers

– and after that? She could not remember.

Perhaps the doll had been left behind in the struggle. It was only too likely – and Elizabeth was too inconsolable to say– No, on reflection she had seen the doll when they were in the wagon. That, then, was where she must search.

She set off at a run back the way they had come towards the courtyard. She met no one until she had crossed the great hall and come to the low stone archway leading to the vaulted passage which gave on to the courtyard by the shortest route. Then she heard voices, two voices raised in anger. She paused, and stole a quick glance into the passage.

She could see no one, but the door of a store room to the right stood open, and the voices came from there. She crept forward cautiously, ready to dart past that open door, but what she heard next drove all thought of her errand from her head.

'...only one course open to us, my lord–' that was Sir Rowland Laverick, his tone reasonable, light-hearted even, but with an underlying nervousness, as if he were trying to persuade his listener to forget some cause for complaint against him. 'With the women and children as hostages he'll give us what terms we choose. So long as we show we mean business.'

'Which I, at least, have already done,' came Lord Devenish's sharp reply.

'All's well that ends well,' put in Sir Rowland nonchalantly, but the words broke off suddenly, as if he had met his companion's angry gaze – Richenda could visualise the scene clearly enough.

'Do you not think, my lord,' he went on more soberly, 'that now is the time to sue for terms, before he has time to bring up his forces for the siege? I would be happy to take the hostages up on to the battlements – under strong guard of course – to show our bargaining power. We could even use force against them, to show we are serious – a damaged limb for every demand refused, perhaps.'

'No!' The vehemence of the reply astonished Richenda. 'Lay one finger on any of them and I'll personally throttle you!'

'B–but, my lord, what use is it if we're not

prepared to back up our demands with force? We might as well not have taken hostages otherwise.'

'We shall make no demands, Laverick. As I said, I'm not crawling for terms to Farrell or anyone else. We defend this place to the limits. And if you want to hope to redeem yourself in my eyes, you can get to work and repair some of the damage you've done before Farrell gets his guns turned on us. Is that clear?'

Richenda smiled to herself, sensing Sir Rowland's discomfort; but there was nothing else to amuse her in Lord Devenish's instructions.

'It's clear to me,' Sir Rowland returned haughtily, 'that you're trying to get back some of the pride you lost at Bristol. It hurt your damned arrogance to march out tamely without so much as a fight, and now you want to save your precious honour by a stupid, suicidal defence here. Well, I'm not risking my neck to save your pride – you can make up your mind to that.'

'For once, Laverick,' Lord Devenish's voice had a dangerous edge to it, 'you'll obey orders to the letter, or I'll place you under arrest. And let me remind you we fought hard at Bristol – and further, that what happened there has nothing to do with us now. I have made my decision, and I expect obedience. So get to work!'

There was a little pause, and then Sir Rowland spoke again in that first ingratiating tone, but a little hesitantly.

'But – my lord – though, I admit, the castle is strong enough to withstand a siege – I ... I must remind you that we have inadequate stores. We cannot hold out for long without food.'

'And whose fault is it, if our stores have not been maintained? The supplies were good when I left, very good – and now I find – well, you know what I find. I'll tell you what we are going to do: we are going to hold this castle until every last bite of food is gone, and every last drop of water, if it comes to that – and then before our last strength has quite left us, we shall ride out and fight with everything that remains to us until we can do no more. Neither I nor any other in this place shall walk out tamely as

Farrell's prisoner.'

'But that's suicide!' Sir Rowland's voice was pitched high with dismay.

'What do you want, then? Humiliation? Penniless exile, living on the charity of some foreign power? To make peace with rebels, submitting to their treasonable demands? No, Laverick, that's not what I want, and it's not what I intend to do.'

'So you'll fight your last battle at Black Castle?' Richenda had asked, only half-seriously; but she had been right, for that was exactly what he intended to do, in a last hopeless, futile, heroic gesture. However fiercely he had denied it just now, she sensed that it had indeed hurt his pride to march unscathed out of Bristol; and here now was his final chance of ending in some kind of glory.

But what, she thought with a shiver, of them? What was to be their part in all this? She could not see that they had ever been necessary to his scheme, if that was what he intended.

It was clear that Sir Rowland shared her bewilderment.

'What of the hostages, then? They'll just be more mouths to feed – what sense is there in that?'

'Farrell will find them here alive and well when he rides into the castle, afterwards,' said Lord Devenish coolly.

'Then why in God's name did you bring them back?' demanded Sir Rowland.

For a moment Lord Devenish was silent, then he said lightly, 'A good question, Laverick – to which I admit I have no answer. But they are here, and they must not be ill-used. And that's my final word on the matter.'

Richenda heard him turn and come towards the door, but she did not move back in time. He saw her at once as he reached the passage. She was reminded, sharply, of that other time outside his room; but except for the immediate circumstances nothing else was the same. She knew from his face – as she had on the journey here – that the game was over, and that now he was in deadly earnest. There was no room for irony, for small meaningless personal triumphs, for taking offence at a mere breach of manners.

He stopped short, his expression sombre and withdrawn, looking down at her.

'What are you doing here?' he demanded sharply.

'I ... I came in search of Elizabeth's doll,' she faltered. 'I think she left it on the wagon.'

'I see – come, then.' He led her in silence into the yard. The doll was there, lying safely on the discarded blankets, a forlorn memento of their journey.

'Thank you,' Richenda said politely, as he handed it to her. She watched him intently for any sign of his old lightness of manner – odd that she should miss his irritating ironical superiority, now that it was no longer there. But anything, she felt, would be better than the bleak eyes which did not seem to see her, the grim line of the fine mouth, the frowning brows. The one des-perate purpose he had spoken of just now seemed to possess him utterly, excluding all else.

But he had not completely forgotten her, for he asked suddenly, 'How much did you hear?'

'I don't know how long you had been talking,' she said, 'but a good deal, I would think.'

'At least then you know how things stand,' he observed briskly. 'Your brother is out there – you know that, of course. The main part of his force should be here in a day or so; with the artillery. They're well equipped.'

'How do you know that?'

'Every commander worth his salt knows his enemy's movements, Mistress Farrell. I've good scouts – I am afraid that while the siege is in progress I must have you all locked up again in one room. I can't afford to spare men to keep watch on you all over the castle – I'll escort you there now, and see to it.'

'Why, my lord,' Richenda asked as they set off, 'do you not save yourself all this trouble and let us go? I can't see that we're any use to you now.'

'I suppose,' he replied, 'because the fighting will be the hotter if your brother knows you're here, in my power: he has more to lose. And I don't relish a half-hearted battle. But I shall see you come to no harm.'

'I think it's stupid!' said Richenda. 'You know you will never win.'

'No, but there are other battles to be fought than the one over who holds Black Castle,' he said, 'and those can be won even in defeat.'

'And now you're talking nonsense,' she retorted bluntly. 'I think men are very foolish, with their ideas of honour and glory and so on. If you weren't all so touchy we'd maybe never have wars at all.'

'Would you have me stand idle when I see my King threatened by a pack of rebels?' he asked proudly.

'I may be a brainless girl,' said Richenda, 'but even I know it was never so simple as that.'

'But then you, Mistress Farrell, are one of the rebels,' he reminded her brusquely.

She could think of no suitable retort to that. They walked on in silence; but at the closed door of Jane's room Lord Devenish paused, his hand on the latch, and turned to her. There was some emotion she could not read mingled with the chilling desolation of his eyes.

'Richenda...' he said, and then he stopped abruptly, and shrugged. 'It doesn't matter.' And he opened the door and ushered her into the room.

Puzzled, disconcerted, she watched him intently as he spoke to Jane with grave courtesy, explaining the necessity for their renewed confinement. But she could see no sign now of whatever it was that had lurked in his eyes outside the door.

Jane had ceased crying now, at last, though her eyes were red, her face blotched and tear-stained. It was very odd, Richenda thought, that the two of them – Jane the prisoner held in the castle while her husband laid siege outside, and Lord Devenish, their triumphant enemy – should look equally unhappy, equally despairing. There was perhaps a certain justice in it.

But now, after what she had heard, Richenda could not find any cause for rejoicing in it, no inclination to taunt him or remind him of his eventual fate. Some of his hopelessness seemed even to have crept into her spirit, though she knew that in the end the future held more hope for the prisoners than for their captor.

He spent some time there, making sure that they knew exactly what they must face: not only their close imprisonment, but the short rations of food which would have to be issued. He did not say that Sir Rowland, by his neglect of the stores, had brought this on them, but he assured them that they would eat at least as well as himself or any of his men.

When he left them at last, Jane turned to Richenda in bewilderment.

'I thought he intended to use us as hostages. What does he mean by all this?'

As well as she could, without letting Jane know why he had made that choice, Richenda told her what she had overheard. It was hard to guess whether they were pleased or sorry to know. After all, as hostages they could hope for the siege to end quickly, to see William again very soon – so long as they were not ill-treated as Sir Rowland had suggested – 'and I thought that he admired you!' exclaimed Jane indignantly at that point in the story.

As simple prisoners in a besieged castle,

desperately held, it might be a very long time before it all ended; but at least they could be fairly sure they would be safe at the end. And since they had no choice in the matter, they could only resign themselves to a long imprisonment here in this small space with little food. It was not a cheering prospect.

It was early the next morning that they first heard the booming roar of William's siege guns.

At the first terrible sound of the guns they were all shocked into silence. The whole solid structure of the castle seemed to shudder, the roar echoed and reverberated about their ears. Jeremy, by the window, wheeling his toy horse, stood still and wide-eyed; Robert awoke and raised his head, looking about him. Jane clasped the bed post, and they all stopped in their tracks to listen.

Elizabeth was the first to speak. 'What was that?' she asked sharply.

'Only the guns, dear,' Jane said as calmly as she could, reaching out trembling hands to comfort the child. She did not say "Your father's guns" – they were confused and frightened enough without that. But she added instead, 'They're not firing at us, only at the bad men. Don't be afraid.' She looked round at the others. 'It's time for morning prayers now,' she said.

They took up their places, standing in a circle, heads bowed devoutly; but as Jane opened her Bible and began to read the guns boomed again, and every word was lost. Elizabeth whimpered and turned to cling to her mother: above her brown head Jane's frightened eyes met Richenda's.

She was trying to be brave, thought Richenda admiringly, for the children's sake if not her own. But she knew how hard it was from her own fast-beating heart. She raised her head and smiled at them all.

'Let's sing a psalm instead, and see if we can make more noise than the guns.'

The suggestion seemed to break the tension, at least among the adults: Jane smiled too, and Nurse took the lead, her strong old voice raised in words designed to keep up their courage:

'The Lord is our defence and aid,
the strength whereby we stand;
When we with woe are much dismay'd
he is our help at hand–'
Jane and Richenda joined her, and slowly, one by one, the children joined in, even Robert's wordless and almost tuneless accompaniment playing its part. They sang as loudly as they could, until the guns seemed to fade to a distant if ominous rumble and they could almost imagine that it was their singing which set the floor trembling beneath their feet.

They sang until they were hoarse, and then in a quiet interval Jane said a short prayer. And then Richenda realised that the whole day stretched ahead of them in this one room with the constant sound of the guns in their ears. There would not even be the distraction of meal times, apart from the scanty supper to be brought to them late in the afternoon: one meal a day was the ration for the garrison and for themselves. Lessons and sewing, they all felt, were not absorbing enough to distract them from the guns.

They took refuge instead in infantile high

spirits. There was little enough space for play, but what there was they used to the full. Richenda gave pick-a-back rides turn by turn to the children, until she was forced to call a halt in laughing exhaustion. Then they played Blind Man's Buff – even Jane and Nurse joining in this – and Hunt-the-Slipper, and all the festival games she could remember from her childhood. An uninformed onlooker might have thought it Jeremy's neglected birthday, or Christmas time, rather than the beginning of a grim siege.

When they had all become thoroughly tired Richenda gathered the children about her and told them a story: not the usual fairy tale, with difficulties overcome and exciting adventures, for she sensed that they did not need any more excitement. Instead she invented a comical tale of a family of white mice, living in luxury in the cellars of a castle and sharing the lives of three human children. It was not easy to leave out any hint of fear and danger, and by the time the story ended she felt she had no powers of inventiveness left; but the children at least were happy.

Then the guard came with their meagre supper.

'Not bread and cheese *again!*' cried Jeremy, as he placed it on the table.

'It'll be plain bread soon,' said the man, 'so make the most of it.'

'Besides,' said Richenda, handing the children their portions, 'it's not bread and cheese – can't you see? Here's your roast venison, Jeremy – and neats' tongues for you, Elizabeth: disguised, of course – and the most delicious syllabub for Robert – marchpane for Mother; and a boar's head, nothing less, for Nurse. Now what have I left for myself?'

'Strawberries and cream!' crowed Jeremy with delight, nearly helpless with laughter. Thank goodness, thought Richenda, that children are so easily amused.

They made a game of everything after that, imagining that the stools were thrones and the bed a royal palace; that Jeremy's horse was a white fairy steed with wings, and Elizabeth's doll their fairy godmother; and that the noise of the guns was the sound of the sea on a far shore where silver ships sailed in a golden sunset. Wrapped in their daydreams, the children went happily and easily to sleep that night.

For a day, perhaps, it was easy enough to keep up their spirits, to distract and entertain, to take the thoughts of the adults from their anxieties by the need to amuse the children. Even for half a day more they could do it. But towards the end of the second day it became harder and harder. Richenda could think of no new, and safe, adventures for her family of mice, and was reduced to repeating what she had already told: the children did not mind that, except that her enthusiasm was flagging too, and they could tell. They tired of the games more quickly today; and their imaginary fairyland lost its novelty; and nothing could convince them today that bread and cheese was anything but hard and stale and unappetising, for all their hunger.

At least at night the guns ceased, and they could rest, but after the first night none of them slept well. On the third day all their courageous high spirits had gone. They were cramped and weary from lack of air and exercise, and too little sleep. They were hungry; and most of all they were thoroughly bored, now that they were back once more with the inadequate diversions of sewing and lessons and the few remaining toys.

That night the guns boomed incessantly, with no quiet spell, no hope of peaceful sleep. If they dozed a little it was in spite of the noise, with its echo continuing in their dreams. By morning they were all thoroughly ill-humoured.

'However long is this going to go on?' demanded Jane of no one in particular. She read them a long passage from the Bible, most of which was drowned by the guns, and they sang, as they had every morning and evening since the siege began. They had reached the final triumphant stanza of Psalm Forty-Six—

'The Lord of hosts doth us defend,
he is our strength and tower;
On Jacob's God we do depend,
and on his mighty power—'
when the door opened abruptly and Lord Devenish came in.

He was dishevelled and grimy, his face lined and shadowed with exhaustion, and he had no time to waste on courtesies.

'The women need help with the wounded,' he said curtly. 'Get down to the great hall and do what you can.'

"The women", they knew, were the camp-followers. As he turned to go Jane drew herself up to her full height and demanded indignantly. 'Do you expect us to keep company with whores?'

Richenda saw the astonishment on his face, and broke in, 'We'll go, my lord – but not Jane. It would be too much for her.'

He did not smile, but there was a slight softening of his expression.

'Thank you,' he said, and was gone.

'Richenda!' Jane protested. 'I meant what I said – you're an innocent, well-born young gentlewoman – you can't go consorting with those soldiers' drabs.'

'I'm not going to consort with them,' said Richenda. 'I'm going to help tend the wounded.'

'Our enemies!' Jane reminded her sharply.

Richenda faced her, with an expression of

unusual gravity.

'Jane,' she said very seriously, 'we have been greatly wronged, but I do not see that it makes our wrong any less if we descend to their level. Let them see that we are not afraid to show them the mercy they denied to us. And,' she added in a near undertone, blushing a little, 'we do pretend to be Christians.'

Jane gazed at her in silence for a moment, and then said gently, 'Sometimes, Richenda, you're so very silly and childish that I despair of you; and sometimes you're so old and wise that I feel ashamed of my own weakness. You're right, of course. I'll come at once.'

Richenda laughed.

'I'm not really all that wise,' she admitted. 'I'm just so bored that any diversion will do. But, Jane, I meant it that you ought not to come – you tire so easily, and you must keep your health or we shall have to nurse you too. That would help no one. And the children need you.'

'That's right,' broke in Nurse. 'You stay with the little ones, madam, and I'll give

Mistress Richenda a hand. I do know a thing or two about caring for the sick, after all. And they may be fiends from the deepest pit of hell, those men out there,' she ended illogically, 'but they are human beings when all's said and done.'

They left Jane, glad to be out of it, with the children and made their way to the great hall. Even before they reached it the stench met them, choking and hideous, catching in the throat.

'We're not a moment too soon, I'd say,' Nurse commented grimly.

The women had done their best, Richenda supposed; but it was hardly enough to meet the needs of the moment. It was clear at once that already the toll taken among the garrison by William's bombardment was high. The wounded had been brought hastily to the hall and laid on the floor, on straw and rough blankets, but the straw must already have been half rotten, and the stink of that alone was enough to turn the stomach. And there seemed to be only three women at work down there, trying desperately to do something for fifteen or more wounded men. They were tired and dishevelled and disorganised, their hands and clothes already dirty and bloodstained, their voices rising shrill with ill-tempered weariness above the groans of the wounded.

Risking the women's resentment, Nurse and Richenda marched in and took control. One woman was set to tear linen for bandages. The most competent, with Nurse's help, to bind wounds, beginning first with the most severely injured; the third to help Richenda in preparing a smaller room adjoining the hall into which the men were carried when they had received attention. 'And then,' said Richenda, 'we can make this place fit for sick men.'

It was already afternoon when the last man had been tended and the hall emptied. They cleared out the straw and set it burning in the courtyard, and then Richenda put them all to work scrubbing the tiled floor of the hall, taking her part with the rest of them, vigorously washing away all trace of blood and filth, flinging open doors and windows and lighting a fire in the hearth so the floor would dry more quickly afterwards. Then they spread clean straw, and went in search of anything fit to make a comfortable bed for a wounded man: which was not easy, after the long weeks of the garrison's occupation.

In the old days the stocks of fresh linen and blankets would never have been allowed to fall so low. But they found what they could and carried it to the hall and made beds along the sides, with room enough between for the women to move freely; and while she worked Richenda remembered grimly the last time she had laid makeshift beds in the hall, and the outcome of that.

And now the men who had raped and looted and murdered here would be brought in to her care, and she must forget what they had done so that she could show them the mercy they had refused to those others. It was better not to think of it at all, but simply to do what was needed as it came her way.

It was as well, perhaps, that while they prepared the hall there seemed to be a temporary lull in the casualties. Most of the wounded had been brought in as a result of the fierce bombardment late in the night, and for now the guns fired only spasmodically. Richenda wondered what damage they had done to the castle, and how William felt at using all his military skill to destroy his own beloved home. It was fortunate that the room they had shared was at the rear of the castle, in the part least open to an assault because it was the most strongly built. At least he would not have to fire on his own wife and children – though she supposed he would not be sure of that. She remembered, wryly, how she had longed for the war to come to Black Castle, and now it was here: civil war in its most painful form.

After that, from the early evening, there was no time for reflection. The bombardment began again more relentlessly than ever, and from here, too, they could hear the answering musket fire from the battlements. Soon, one by one – and then in twos and threes – the wounded were carried into the hall. There was more than enough now for them to do: wounds to be cleansed and bandaged, shattered limbs to be set and bound, splintered fragments of wood and tiny pieces of stone to be extracted, sleeping draughts to be given to men racked with pain, the comfort of a quiet word and a soothing touch for the frightened or anxious.

Richenda and Nurse and the three women worked on through the night, seeing nothing but the task to be done, unaware of time passing or of anything beyond these walls. It was easy now to forget what these men had done, and see only their need and their suffering.

Soon after dawn Lord Devenish came briefly to the hall. He paused in the doorway, his eyes taking in the quiet orderliness which filled the room, and then he set out, passing from bed to bed, talking to the sick men. Richenda could see no trace now in his expression or his manner of the despair there had been before: only an air of concentration, of absorption in the needs of the moment, even of a certain quiet enjoyment as far as the suffering around him allowed.

After a time he came to where Richenda

knelt in the straw, replacing a bandage which had come loose on a man's arm. She paused and looked up at him, and he nodded at her.

'You've worked wonders here,' he said quietly, rather in the tone of an indulgent schoolmaster commending an apt pupil. 'Well done.' And then he moved on to talk to the man in the next bed.

Her task done, she sat back on her heels and watched his progress down the hall. She was struck once more with the commanding grace of his presence, with the way in which all around shrank to insignificance when he was there. His face haggard with weariness and grey with dust, his clothes torn and disreputable, his voice roughened with shouting against the noise of the guns, he was yet every inch the proud leader of men.

And more than that, Richenda realised, watching the men's faces as he spoke to them, seeing them smile through their pain and follow him with their eyes as he moved away from them. They loved him, she realised. Amazingly, astonishingly, they loved him. Yet if it were not for him, for his desperate decision to fight to the end, they would not be here now, any of them. She wondered if they knew that, and if it would make any difference if they did.

She saw him pause to speak with Nurse – was she too receiving that schoolmasterly praise? – and then he left them. It was then she recognised suddenly that something had gone from her feeling for him, something she had thought would always be there, something which without doubt she still had every reason to feel: she no longer hated him.

She wanted his defeat, of course, for without it they would never be free; but she wanted it calmly, dispassionately, because it had to be and not with the fierce loathing of before.

The day passed in ceaseless work: it was hot outside, and even here in the high-roofed hall it became oppressive. The men cried out for water and threw aside their blankets. And always as they worked the noise of the guns echoed clamorously through their heads and set the very foundations trembling. It did not help the men's recovery, or the calmness of their nurses; but they carried on as best they could, scarcely pausing to eat their inadequate rations.

At some time about midday one of the women fainted, from heat or hunger or sleeplessness or overwork – or more likely all four of them, Richenda suspected. She was carried away to bed, and the four of them who were left worked on: five, Richenda knew, had really been too few for the task.

A little after that two soldiers carried in a third and laid him in a space near the door: a familiar enough sight by now, but Richenda sensed as she went to meet them that this time it was a little different.

'Don't think there's much chance for him,' said one of the bearers.

Richenda bent over the man, suppressing a horrified exclamation at the dreadful open wound in his chest, and laid her fingers on his pulse; and then she saw, at the moment when she knew he was dead, that it was Dick Price.

She looked up at the man who had

spoken. 'He's dead,' she said simply. 'I knew him.'

The man nodded. 'He died bravely: threw himself in my lord's path when the shot hit the wall up there, and took the full blast on himself. My lord will be sorry he's gone.'

Richenda looked down at the still face. It no longer looked quite like the face she knew so well, a little shrunken already, and waxen, the eyes not quite closed. Dick Price, who had betrayed them twice, who had been willing for money to destroy the trust and affection built up over a lifetime.

Yet it could not have been quite so simple as that, in the end: why otherwise had he stayed with Lord Devenish, certainly penniless now, defeated, fighting hopelessly for a lost cause? Self-interest should long ago have driven Dick Price away, if not back to his old master then at least to the winning side. It was not lack of opportunity which had kept him where his disloyalty had led him, for times without number he could have escaped if he had chosen.

And now, inexplicably, he had given his life for the man who above all knew the worst he could do. Richenda remembered at that moment the devotion on the faces of the wounded as they gazed at Lord Devenish: first that, and now this. What kind of man was he, who could act so cruelly and so ruthlessly, speak with such uncaring cynicism; and yet without effort inspire a man to die for him?

The question remained unanswered. She rose to her feet, with a last look at the dead face of Dick Price, whose squalid life had ended so nobly, who could perhaps once have answered her question.

Then they carried him away, to the room where the dead were laid.

CHAPTER ELEVEN

By the following morning they had nearly thirty men on their hands, many of them feverish and gravely ill. That day three men died, as two had the day before. And by now, too, Nurse had a tense grey-faced look about her which filled Richenda with consternation when she saw it.

'You must go and rest, Nurse,' she urged, 'or you'll not be able to carry on at all.'

She realised then that the old woman was looking at her with just the same attentive expression of concern as must be on her own face. Did she, too, look so exhausted? Nurse smiled.

'I was just going to say the same to you, Mistress Richenda.'

'Then I suppose we both need rest – but we can't both be spared at once. You go and sleep now, and then I'll take my turn. That seems sensible.'

She was afraid Nurse would argue that she herself should go first; but after a moment the old woman agreed and made her slow way from the room, promising to be back as soon as she could. At least the woman who had fainted – whenever it was, she had lost track of the days – had returned now, and the other women had taken turns to rest; so they were not desperate without Nurse.

But it was bad enough, for Nurse with her lifetime's experience was worth two of the rest of them. Many times that day, faced with a difficult wound or a dangerously feverish patient, Richenda missed the reassurance of the old woman's approval and advice.

Lord Devenish came again that morning, as he had yesterday, cheering the men, praising the women. Richenda thought, watching him, that it was as if he brought a breath of life into this place of sickness, warm, vigorous purposeful life, in every line of his strong lithe body, in every note of his deep resonant voice. Even dust and weariness could not quench that intrinsic vitality. And he still had the power, as he paused to speak to her, of setting every sense tingling with a glance of those grey eyes.

'You must rest soon, Mistress Farrell,' he remarked gently today. He had never spoken to her in quite that tone before, with such concern: she felt the colour rise in her tired face, and could not answer for a moment.

'I'll rest when my turn comes, my lord,' she said at last, and he smiled briefly and was gone.

Mercifully the rest of that day was a quiet one, as the days went now: only one new patient was carried in, and he only slightly hurt. It gave them time to see to the needs of the men already there. Almost always fever set in after the first day, and if the men survived the wound the fever often took them instead. There was little any of them could do but soothe and comfort, and give drinks of cool water.

'At least the food'll last longer this way,' one of the camp-followers said, dryly, as she closed the eyes of a newly dead man and set off in search of two soldiers to carry the body away.

It might be a harsh comment, Richenda thought, but they could not allow room for sentiment here. Pause for one moment, and think of the wounds and the suffering and the waste of life, and one would go mad. Better far to be a little detached from it all, calm, cool, efficient and uninvolved.

Perhaps it was just because of those qualities that Richenda had learned to regard the camp-followers with respect. They had known all the hardships of campaign life, starved or feasted as the fortunes of their menfolk changed, shared good times and bad without complaint, expecting neither compliments nor thanks nor commendation. Now they worked ceaselessly, uncomplainingly, at whatever was asked of them, with a good humour and practical common sense which, Richenda had to admit, often exceeded her own. Never again would she be tempted to look on them with a sense of her own superiority.

By the evening she knew she had almost come to the end of her strength. She could barely stand, dizzy as she was for lack of sleep; when the food came she was scarcely able to eat, though she ought to have been hungry. She began to watch the door, when she could, for any sign of Nurse returning. Soon, perhaps, as they were so quiet for the moment, she might see if they could manage without her and snatch a few hours' sleep upstairs. She knew she would work better for it.

She had almost taken that decision when the sound of a commotion somewhere outside reached them, and they heard agitated voices and hurrying steps; and another wounded man was carried into the hall.

She knew who it was before his name reached her, passed in whispers from man to man across the room. Some instinct, sharp and chilling, told her, setting her stomach turning in sick awareness before the woman at her side gave a gasp and said, 'It's my lord himself!'

They laid him on a blanket in a corner of the hall, where there was space – there was little enough left by now – and Richenda ran to him, with a terrible anguish tearing at her. The other women drew back and let her pass as if she alone, by virtue of her skill and her unspoken authority, had the right to attend him.

She heard them saying how the blast from a cannon shot had struck him as he stood on the battlements – no Dick Price to take the force of it now – and thrown him back on to the wall behind in a shower of scattered stone and splintered woodwork. As they spoke she looked down at him lying there, grey-faced and motionless with blood trickling over his forehead from the dark line of his hair and a dreadful mangled wound in his right shoulder and chest and forearm.

She forgot all about the need to be calm and detached and almost cried out, so great was her pain. And then she saw how they were watching her, waiting for her to give him the same controlled attention as she had shown to every other man she had tended. So she took a deep breath and tried to still the trembling of her hands, and knelt down at his side.

The head wound first, in case that was the worst of the two. She ran her fingers, gently probing, through the thick curls of his hair: and as she did so he gave a low moan. He moved his head and opened his eyes, gazing straight into hers.

'My turn now,' he said very faintly, with a movement of the lips which might have been an attempt at a smile. It was almost as hard for Richenda to force her accustomed reassuring, smile to her own lips, for her eyes were full of tears.

'That's right,' she said, her voice emerging as a hoarse whisper because of the painful lump in her throat.

At least the head wound seemed to be slight. Thank God for that! It could wait until she'd attended to the shoulder.

She turned to the ghastly sickening mess which the blast had made through the thickness of buff coat and shirt, all torn bleeding flesh and splintered bone and jagged fragments of wood and stone. If it had touched his lung—!

She raised her eyes to his face and saw that he was still watching her, with that little hint of a smile through the pain.

'I'm afraid I shall have to take out the splinters and things,' she said gently. 'It will hurt you: I'm sorry.'

She turned to ask one of the waiting soldiers to bring the improvised tools they used, and saw that the women were there still, their faces pale and anxious: like the soldiers they too loved him, for he treated them with a courtesy of a kind they rarely met with.

'There are other sick men who need you,' she reminded them quietly, understanding their reluctance to go.

It was the two soldiers who brought the tools and stood to watch and to help as she set to work. Her hands must not shake now, when it mattered so much! She heard his sharp intake of breath as she began, and his eyes closed: she must be as quick and as neat as she could.

She worked steadily, cutting away the sleeve and what was left of his coat, removing the fragments piece by piece from the wound, trying desperately to make nothing worse by her efforts. But she must not be long, for the blood was draining slowly but steadily into the blankets, staining her hands and forearms and her skirts, and every moment taking his strength with it.

She finished at last and set to work to bind the wound firmly with the makeshift bandages which were all they had, and to raise and support the arm in a sling across his damaged chest. A simple bandage served for the head wound, and then she felt his pulse and listened anxiously to his breathing. A weak rapid pulse, and breathing already quick and shallow; but it was not laboured, nor was he coughing blood, as men did when the lung was injured, before they died – not yet, at least.

She raised him a little with the help of one of the soldiers and slid a folded blanket beneath his head and shoulders, and then she laid another blanket gently over him. When she had finished she saw that he was conscious again, his eyes open.

'All done with now,' she assured him softly. His dry lips moved, but she could not hear what he tried to say. 'Would you like some water?' she asked.

A faint movement of his head answered her, and she brought a cup of water to him supporting him on her arm as she held it to his mouth.

'Thank you,' he whispered afterwards.

'Now see if you can sleep,' she said.

His eyes closed and he lay still, and she knelt there at his side for a long time, watching him. He ought not to be left, she was sure of that: just for fear he took a turn for the worse. She did not in any case think she could have stood up now if she had wanted to, for every movement brought on the exhausted dizziness she had forgotten in the moment of crisis. From time to time her head jerked suddenly forward and she knew she had almost fallen asleep.

Then after a while Lord Devenish grew restless, and she gave him more water and anxiously felt his pulse. But it was the pain which kept him wakeful, she could see that as he shifted uncomfortably, finding a moment's rest perhaps when she smoothed the blanket beneath his head or straightened his covers or brought him a drink; and then in a minute or two lying again in silent endurance, with that line of pain between his brows which she longed to be able to smooth away.

In the end she brought him a sleeping draught, and watched him gently slide into a deep and peaceful sleep; and then she sat on for a long time – she did not know how long – in a kind of daze, her gaze lingering on the strong lines of his face, tanned still beneath the greyness. The dark lashes – long lashes – curved on the sharply defined cheekbones, the mouth was gentle in repose above the firm chin; and then the hands, wide, brown, long fingered, the left relaxed on the rough blanket, the other concealed in the sling.

Sebastian Devenish, who for so long had held them in his power, to use as he chose; the man she had hated with all the intensity of her youth; the man whose vitality had struck her so sharply in this very place the other day, who against her will could turn her limbs to water with a glance. That man was now brought to this, the suffering human being who needed her. The pity of it tore at her heart.

Then at last she became dimly aware that someone was beside her, and a hand touched her shoulder.

'Mistress Richenda, I'm back now: I've had a good long rest. Now off you go and sleep, before we have to carry you there.'

Richenda looked up, her thoughts far away, and it took her a moment or two to remember who was the old woman at her side, and what she was talking about.

'I can't leave him,' she said, pressing her hands to her eyes, hoping to be able to see more clearly afterwards through the mist of weariness.

'Nonsense,' Nurse said briskly. 'He's sleeping like a babe. Get yourself up those stairs now.'

Richenda did not move. 'But he might get worse.'

'Then I'll be here, never you worry.' Nurse paused suddenly, struck by some new thought, and looked closely at Richenda. 'I thought you hated him,' she said sharply.

'No, not now, not any more,' mumbled Richenda; and then she saw what was in

Nurse's eyes, read there the truth she had not recognised until now.

She had reflected the other day that her hate had gone, that she had learned to view him calmly, dispassionately, as a man like any other, who happened by some mischance to have crossed her path.

But it was not anything so cool as an absence of hate which had brought her to his side tonight, which had driven her on in spite of exhaustion and hunger to care for him more devotedly, watch him more anxiously, than she had any other man in that hall. It was not an absence of hate which had filled her with anguish and pity and grief and driven away the detachment on which she depended. It was not an absence of hate which kept her here now, when every bone in her aching body cried out for rest.

It was love.

Stupid, hopeless love, as futile as his wish to hold Black Castle to the end. For what could come of it? What possible happiness or satisfaction could it offer her? True, he had held her once in his arms and her body had come alive at his touch as never before; true, he had told her she was – what was the phrase? – 'damned attractive'. But there was no hope for her in either of those memories. Like any other soldier, a pretty woman excited him, and she knew, without vanity, that she was pretty. That was all.

Never, at any other time, had he shown anything but exasperation with her, except just lately when he had praised her work here in this room – and that was only because, like Nurse and the other women, she was useful to him. It was as much as she could ever hope for.

Love! It was supposed to mean joy and laughter and delightful stolen kisses; dancing feet and a light and carefree heart; moments of passion and sweetness and shared delight. But all she had now was a heavy ache, a dull pain, that was at once an emptiness and a constant burden. Richenda bent her head and bit her lip to keep the tears at bay.

And then she took herself in hand. This was foolish, to let her silly wayward heart drive out all her common sense, just when she needed it most. It had happened, she knew that now. She must accept it – had accepted it – and then put it out of her head and get on with the business of living. It would be a useless waste of time and emotion to dwell on what could not be. She had no patience, she told herself, with such needless self-indulgence.

She raised her head and swallowed her tears and straightened her shoulders, and then allowed Nurse to help her to her feet. She even managed a wan and tremulous smile.

'I'll do as I'm told then, and go to bed.'

And with only one parting glance at the man she loved, she made her unsteady way upstairs.

Richenda did not remember afterwards how she had found her way to Jane's room and into bed. She only knew that much, much later she woke after a long and dreamless sleep to find the sun streaming through the windows on to the honey-coloured boards of the floor, and wondered where she was, and how she came to be there.

Her eyes followed the shaft of sunlight

until it came to rest on Elizabeth's demure brown person, sewing with frowning concentration on her low stool; and then moved on to Jeremy, gazing unenthusiastically and ineffectively at his Latin Grammar; and Robert with his thumb in his mouth, returning her gaze with solemn blue eyes. But it was not until she saw Jane in her high-backed chair, her hands still for once, the sewing neglected on her lap while she stared mournfully into the unseen distance, that she remembered who they all were.

Of course, she was at Black Castle, in Jane's room, and they were in the hands of their enemies. She remembered that scene in the hall – and herself in the garden alone, at the mercy of those men. That was why she was in bed, resting – but where was Mary; and Nurse? That wasn't it, after all...

'How long have I been asleep?' she asked, breaking into Jane's unhappy reflections.

'All night,' said Jane, looking round sharply, 'and most of today. It's well into the afternoon now.' She laid aside her sewing and came with gentle concern to the bedside.

'All night'. Last night – yes, she knew now – the grey face drawn with pain, the dreadful wound. Richenda's heart gave a great lurch and she pushed aside the covers and swung her feet to the floor. In a moment Jane had grasped her arm.

'Don't get up yet, Richenda. Rest while you can. I'll bring you something to eat in bed.'

Richenda gazed up at her in anguish.

'But I ought to go back. I might be needed.'

All those hours of sleep, and anything could have happened – he would have woken long since – no, she had no time to eat.

'Don't be silly, Richenda,' Jane insisted firmly. 'They've managed without you so far. They can manage for half an hour longer, until you've eaten. You'll be better for it.'

And then the last piece fell into place, the final recollection of last night, of that stark moment of awareness at Lord Devenish's side. Common-sense, self-control, that was what she had known last night that she must cultivate. Richenda took a deep breath and forced herself to return to bed, and to eat, unenthusiastically, the food Jane brought her.

'They say Lord Devenish was wounded yesterday,' observed Jane conversationally, sitting on the bed whilst Richenda ate. 'Sir Rowland Laverick has taken charge in his place.'

'Oh yes?' Richenda said as casually as she could, her head bent so Jane should not see her face.

'Perhaps he'll end the siege,' went on Jane.

Richenda paused in her eating, struck by this new idea, then she rejected it. 'Not if he had orders to the contrary,' she said with conviction. 'He'd not dare.'

She saw that her words had depressed Jane a little, destroyed some small hope which had been taking shape.

'Don't forget what he wanted to do to us,' she reminded Jane.

'Yes, I suppose that's true,' said Jane. 'But how long will it go on? Does William have to batter the castle round our ears before they give in?'

'I think they intended to ride out and fight before then,' said Richenda, growing impatient with this fruitless speculation. She ate the last mouthful of cheese and brushed the crumbs from the embroidered silk counterpane. 'Well, I've eaten all up like a good girl,' she said. 'Can I go now?' She did not feel as light-hearted as her words suggested.

Jane laughed.

'Of course you may – but are you sure you wouldn't rather I took your place?'

Richenda shook her head vehemently.

'No! – No, it wouldn't be right for you, Jane. Much better you stay here.'

She stayed just long enough to exchange her blood-stained gown for a severe but practical smock of brown holland, and then made her way to the door, forcing herself to walk more slowly than her anxious spirit urged. Halfway there she realised that something familiar, something which had been part of the background to their lives during the past days, had gone.

'The guns have stopped,' she said.

'Yes,' said Jane. 'I haven't heard them at all

since late morning. I don't know why.'

Richenda found she did not greatly care; and went on her way, putting the thought from her mind. Not too fast, head high, she walked along the passage, only the wild anxious beating of her heart was beyond her control.

She came to the gallery, glancing down. Everything seemed exactly as it had before: the neat rows of beds, the atmosphere of busy quietness. From here she could not see him.

Down the stairs, one, two, three, four ... fifteen, sixteen. 'No,' she thought, 'I must not run in front of them all.' She turned under the gallery, returned a greeting from one of the camp-followers and answered a cheerful comment from a soldier who was almost well now.

There, there in the corner, against the wall, with Nurse bent over so she could not see his face: only a restless movement of the feet beneath the blanket to show he was still alive. For a moment she paused, and closed her eyes with relief.

When she opened them again Nurse had

turned her head to speak to one of the women, asking for something to be brought, perhaps. Her face was flushed, anxious, harassed. Richenda's breath caught in her throat, and she did run then, the last few yards to where Nurse knelt in the straw. Before she reached him she could hear his low, incoherent, rambling speech.

Lord Devenish's eyes were open, but whatever they saw it was nothing in that hall. His head moved restlessly beneath the cold compress Nurse held to his forehead; his lips moved endlessly, the words making no sense. His sound hand reached out, gesturing, grasping at the air. High spots of colour on the lean cheekbones, eyes too bright, seeing too much – Richenda gave a low cry and sank on the straw at Nurse's side.

'How long has he been like this?' she asked.

Nurse turned her head.

'Since early this morning. Though he's only been wandering the last few hours or so.'

Richenda laid her fingers on his wrist, to

feel the throbbing pulse. 'He's burning hot, Nurse. Oh, what can we do?'

'Same as we've done for all of them when the fever sets in,' Nurse said sensibly. 'Water to drink, and a cold compress. And make sure he doesn't open that wound with thrashing about.' She gazed keenly at Richenda. 'Have you slept well?'

'Yes, of course.' She brushed the question aside, as of no importance.

'And eaten?'

Richenda nodded.

'Right then, I'll leave you here and go and give a hand with that lad over there: looks as though he may lose a leg. Nell there's gone for some more water.'

Richenda slid into Nurse's place and bent over Lord Devenish to hold the compress in place. In spite of it, she could see the sweat trickling from his face into his hair, darkening the bright curls. She was alone with him, as alone as she could be in this crowded room.

'Oh my love,' she whispered, knowing that he could not hear her, 'please get well, my darling – that's all I ask, just for you to be well again. Nothing else, love, nothing else at all..'

She laid her free hand over his, gently caressing; and then her heart gave a great lurch as his fingers turned and grasped hers in a hold so strong it was almost painful. But there was no recognition in his eyes, only a momentary look of panic, and he cried out some word of command to an imaginary troop, clutching her hand as if it were the hilt of a sword.

'Hush, my darling, hush now.' Gently she smoothed the damp curls of his hair from his face, and straightened the makeshift pillow. Nell brought the water, and she filled the cup Nurse had left, and then slid her arm under his shoulders and raised him a little to drink.

He sipped at the water, clearly thankful for its refreshing coolness, and then turned his head against her breast. For a moment she bent and laid her lips on his burning forehead, and held him close. It could do no harm when he did not know what was happening, would not remember afterwards – if there was an afterwards.

Then she laid him gently down and soaked the compress in the water and held it again to his head.

So it went on for the last hours of the day, through the long night. Richenda bathed his face and hands, gave him water to drink, smoothed his covers; and talked on in a low voice, telling him of her love, willing him to grow well, saying all the things she could never, ever say if she knew he could hear. The delirium never lessened, though at times the mutterings grew quieter. Low-voiced, anxious, hurried, inaudible phrases, poured out; at other times he shouted, cried out, gave orders as if on the battlefield. Then, once, towards morning, he fell briefly silent, and when he spoke again it was distinctly, unmistakably, 'Richenda–'

She took his hand and bent over him, her heart beating fast.

'My darling?' she whispered. His eyes were on her face, wide and dark. She held her breath with hope,

'Richenda...' His brows drew together in a frown, his head moved restlessly from side to side. 'No, no,' he muttered. 'There's no way... It doesn't matter, it doesn't matter.'

The words trailed into incoherence; she saw that he did not know her, never had known her.

She bent her head on to the pillow, the tears rising to her eyes with bitter disappointment. She remembered when he had spoken her name once before, outside Jane's room: absent-mindedly, forgetting the courtesy which required the correct formality of 'Mistress Farrell'. It had been nothing more than a moment of inattention: now he lived through it again in his delirium–

Gradually his restless activity subsided. He lay still, talking rarely, and then in so low a voice that she scarcely knew he had spoken. Often he lapsed into an uneasy sleep which was closer to stupor than healthy slumber. His pulse, when she felt it, was clearly weakening, faint and slow, and his breathing so quiet, so shallow she wondered once or twice if it had ceased altogether.

Nurse came once to see how he was, and shook her head. 'He'll be lucky to come out of this alive,' she said, with a clumsy pat of Richenda's shoulder by way of comfort.

There was nothing much anyone could do, but moisten his lips from time to time, and watch and wait. And there were other sick men who were not beyond help. Reluctantly, Richenda left Lord Devenish's side and went to do what she could for the others, in a torment of anxiety until she could return again to that other bedside and reassure herself that he was still alive.

At last, late in the day, she could confidently say that there was nothing more for her to do, and resume her place at his side with a clear conscience. Lord Devenish lay motionless now, his eyes closed, his face drained of colour. She knelt with her fingers on his failing pulse, watching, waiting for the outcome she so deeply dreaded, trying not to think, nor to hope, with a kind of wordless prayer running through her.

She did not know how long she had been there when she sensed a change, an almost imperceptible movement of his hand, a small sighing breath. She looked up and saw that his eyes were open: not darkened with fever now, but clear, intelligent, watching her.

His lips moved, but no words came. She reached up to lay a hand on his forehead and found it cool to her touch: beneath her other hand his fingers moved, very slightly. Then he turned his head a little towards her, and his eyes closed; and his breathing was the quiet even breathing of a weary man, sleeping at last.

Richenda bent her head on her arms and wept in a passion of relief and thankfulness.

She could rest herself then, stretched on the prickly straw at his side, her cheek resting on her hand, sleeping lightly and peacefully knowing that all was well; but ready at any moment to wake if he needed her.

Elsewhere in the hall the others were resting too, leaving one of their number always awake and alert for an emergency. No new patients had been carried in all day, and only one the day before: the silence of the guns explained that readily enough. Some of the sick men had recovered sufficiently to leave their beds, and three more had died: one the man whose gangrenous leg had been amputated last night. Now, if there were no fresh casualties, they could manage the nursing easily between them.

It was in the dark hour before dawn that Richenda heard a soft movement from the bed, and sat up quickly. Torches set in sconces on the walls gave a restless uncertain light, but she could see Lord Devenish clearly enough as she bent over him. He was looking up at her, and he was smiling, a sweet, warm boyish smile which set her pulses racing as if it were she now who had the fever. And then with an effort he reached up, slowly, unsteadily with his sound arm and very lightly touched her cheek.

'Richenda,' he whispered.

CHAPTER TWELVE

She closed her eyes, scarcely believing what she had heard, and imprisoned his hand in both of hers. When she looked again he was still smiling.

'I'm here,' she said gently. She wanted to add 'my love,' but she dared not. He had called her by name, but that might not mean anything: she must not let herself hope that it did. Better to be practical. 'Could you manage to eat something?'

His fingers moved to curve around hers; his eyes rested still on her face.

'Later,' he said. And then: 'Richenda, I think I have always loved you.'

The words were quiet, soft as a breeze; but she heard them, and for a moment the room seemed to sway about her, the torches to bend drunkenly. No, she thought; it cannot be right.

'What did you say?' she breathed.

He gave a faint laugh.

'You heard,' he told her teasingly.

'But I don't understand–'

'Don't you?' Sebastian Devenish smiled again. 'I have never in all my life loved until now,' he went on in that same soft low voice. 'I thought love was not for me, and then I saw you – and there will never be anyone else as long as I live–'

She knelt with eyes closed, his hand clasped to her breast, and wanted that low tender voice to go on and on. 'I had no hope of anything – I thought you had only hatred for me – and then, in my sickness, I seemed to see you there, hear you speaking, saying what I never hoped to hear you say. Was it real, Richenda, or did I just dream it?'

She smiled, a great wide foolish smile which could not hope to contain the leaping joy of her heart.

'No, my darling, you did not dream it. I said it all, every word – only I did not think you knew–' She laughed, because she could not help it. 'I cannot believe it's true.'

'Nor I,' he returned wonderingly. 'What have I ever done to deserve this? – Nothing

I can think of – ' He was silent, gazing at her in deep contentment; but she could see that all the talking had tired him, and remembered that he had eaten nothing as yet.

'You lie quiet now,' she said gently, 'and I'll bring you something to eat.'

'Something' for the men newly recovered from fever, was stale bread soaked in water; which had made Richenda think longingly, more than once, of the delicate broths Nurse had taught her to make when there was more than bread and cheese in the larder. Now she brought the unappetising mess to him in a bowl, more regretful than ever, and knelt down to give it to him.

'I'm sorry that's all there is,' she said sadly.

Sebastian smiled.

'From your hands, dear heart, it is ambrosia,' he said extravagantly.

She laughed, and laid down the bowl while she slid her arm behind his shoulders to raise him. Not this time as the nurse, conscious of his need; but aware instead of the broad back, the smooth skin, of his nearness. In a moment, somehow, he had his sound arm about her and had pulled her close until her head rested on his shoulder, his mouth on her hair. She could feel the beating of his heart against her, the unexpected strength of his arm.

'I am not helpless, Richenda,' he told her softly. 'Not quite, that is – look at me.'

Obediently she raised her head, and her lips met the warm firmness of his mouth as his arm drew her closer to lie against him on the bed, his hand running caressingly along the curve of her back. She slid her fingers into the thickness of his hair, and felt again that melting sweetness in her limbs, that longing to be held closer and closer, to feel the hard lines of his body against her, to become one with him, to be possessed, completely and wholly.

But in a moment his hold slackened about her, and his mouth moved away from hers.

'Steady, dear heart – I can't–' He was breathless now, eyes closed, his face white, and she bent over him full of compunction.

'My darling, I'm sorry – I was forgetting–' With relief she saw the colour return slowly to his face, and he gave her a rueful smile.

'How stupid, not to be able to hold you as I wish—'

'If you would only let me give you this horrible stuff then you'd get your strength back much more quickly,' she reproved laughingly.

This time he ate his way through the unappealing concoction, slowly, with many pauses to smile at her, to share their new-found joy in each other.

'I have never known anyone like you,' he commented once.

She laughed, and he went on: 'No, I meant it in a good sense. You are such a slight little thing, as beautiful and fragile – looking as one of those little blue flowers one sees sometimes on the road—'

'Periwinkles?' suggested Richenda.

'Very likely,' he said with a smile. 'Yet you are stubborn and strong-willed, and you can take charge of a hospital – or an escape – without a moment's hesitation. I'm amazed your brother didn't take you to war with him.'

'Yes,' Richenda agreed brightly. 'I'd have made a good camp-follower.' And then realised what implication he might read into her words, and blushed. She saw that he had finished eating, and to cover her confusion took the bowl from him. 'You ought to try and sleep now,' she said.

'I will, if you'll stay with me,' he said. He held out his hand. 'Come here.'

She stayed where she was, on her knees, watching him.

'You're not strong yet, remember,' she said warningly.

'I remember,' he said. 'I just want you to lie here beside me.'

She allowed him to draw her close again, held in the crook of his arm on the blanket at his side, her head in the hollow of his shoulder as if it had been made for that very place. He touched her hair briefly with his lips, and gave a sigh of contentment.

'Now I can sleep,' he said. 'And you, too, my dear heart.'

Nurse found them when she came that way soon after dawn, sleeping peacefully in each others' arms; and she pursed her lips and shook her head in vehement disapproval.

'No good will come of that!' she muttered to herself before she left them.

When Richenda opened her eyes it was as if she awoke to find by some miracle that her deepest dream of happiness had become reality. There, looking into hers as she lay at his side, were Sebastian's grey eyes, tender, full of all the love he had declared to her in the night. His arm was about her, holding her as if he meant that nothing again should ever part them. He smiled at her, that sweet heart-stopping smile which was so new to her.

'Good morning, my dear heart,' he whispered, and she reached up to answer him gently, tenderly, with a kiss.

Last night it had been as if they were alone, in the dim light while the others slept. Now there was a bustle of activity as dressings were changed, water carried in, the fire revived, and there were curious glances cast at the pair in the corner.

Somehow it was accepted, unquestioningly, that they had a need for each other which no one who saw it would wish to deny. Nurse might look sour and disapproving, but even she made no comment to Richenda as she came to work alongside the others, with dancing eyes and light feet and a glow of ecstasy about her which nothing there could dim.

Lord Devenish slept and woke by turns, his face lit with joy when she came to him, as she did often, to see how he was; impatient when she left him, for however short a time. If he could not sleep, and she seemed to be too closely occupied elsewhere for his liking, he would send her some trivial request to bring her back to his side. And then they would talk and laugh, or simply be quiet together in deep and perfect happiness.

It was about midday, as Richenda was taking water to a patient at the fireside, that one of the women came yet again to say that my lord was asking for her. She smiled, but went on with her task, and only when her patient was settled comfortably crossed the hall on quiet but tripping feet to that shadowy corner.

'My lord summoned me?' she asked with a

teasing smile.

'You kept me waiting, wench,' he said, and held up his arm to draw her to him. He was sitting up now, propped on pillows, and she nestled close at his side.

'I've work to do,' she returned demurely. 'I can't be always at your beck and call.'

'The falcon always comes at the call of the lure,' he said.

'Not this falcon!' she protested indignantly. 'You forget I escaped you, once at least.'

'Not quite, my little bird, not quite.'

'And not again, ever,' she said, relenting. She felt him shiver, and he said quickly:

'Don't, my dear heart! Don't think of "ever", or of anything but now: it's better that way.'

She looked up at him, puzzled by his tone.

'I only say what I feel, my lord,' she said.

'The name is Sebastian,' he said. 'It sounds more friendly – and say what you feel, if you must, only let it be what you feel here and now, and no more.'

'What–?' she began, but he silenced her with a kiss.

'No questions, dear heart. Let it rest.'

She was silent for a moment, and then she said, 'What made you love me? I was so rude to you.' She felt her colour rising at the memory.

'I think that was exactly why,' he replied with a quiet laugh. 'That proud, stubborn spirit of yours, that indomitable courage: my brave, resourceful, most beloved Richenda. Perhaps it is merely self-preservation on my part to love you. Better far to have you as a friend than an enemy.'

She smiled up at him.

'Do you know, I think I love you for much the same reason. I thought that was why I hated you, but I don't think it was ever really hate. What a well-matched pair we are.'

'Flint and stone, to draw fire, the one from the other. Yes, ideally matched, my dear heart.' He bent as if to kiss her, and then paused. 'We have a visitor.'

She turned to follow his gaze. At the foot of the gallery stairs a soldier stood, looking their way, as if unsure of his next move. Then as one of the women passed he spoke to her, his gestures indicating themselves, and after a moment she came to the bedside.

'Mistress Farrell, that man asks for a word with you.'

'Let him come here,' said Lord Devenish. 'Mistress Farrell is not to be ordered around.'

'Except by you,' Richenda amended in an undertone.

The woman took the message, and returned almost at once. 'He insists, Mistress Farrell, that he must speak with you alone.'

Lord Devenish frowned.

'What insolence! That is one of my own men–'

'Never mind,' said Richenda soothingly. 'Perhaps he wishes to enquire after you, and thinks he'll have a fuller answer from me. I'll go and see.'

He let her go then, with a lingering clasp of the hand.

As she reached him, the man grasped Richenda's arm, and she stiffened. 'Sir Rowland Laverick wants you upstairs,' he said.

Her eyes widened. 'Wants me? But why?'

'That's his orders. That's all I can tell you.'

'But I have work to do here. And I don't wish to come.'

His grasp on her arm tightened. 'You have no choice, mistress.'

She looked round at Lord Devenish and saw his eyes on her, frowning at what he saw of the man's manner: she must not worry him, so newly recovered.

'Very well,' she said, 'I will come. But release my arm.'

He did so after a moment, and she went with him up the stairs, along the passages to that room in the gatehouse tower which Lord Devenish had made his office.

Only now another man had made it his, lounging at ease in the carved chair behind the wide oak table. Sir Rowland Laverick, as elegantly dressed in satin and lace as if he had never been near a battlefield. At the other side of the table were ranged six people: Jane and the children, under the guard of another soldier; and seated in another carved chair, the familiar but by now almost forgotten figure of Master Stephen Pritchard, William's household chaplain, whom they had last seen riding out with William himself after that last visit so long ago.

'Master Pritchard!' Richenda exclaimed. 'What–? I don't understand...' She looked about in bewilderment.

Her first thought, a natural one after all that had happened, was of treachery; that even the chaplain had betrayed his trust.

And then she saw the document on the table, a long parchment roll, held flat by an inkwell and a stone and Sir Rowland's white hand. It was closely written in numbered paragraphs, and laid ready beside it the sealing wax and a new quill. Richenda had never seen a treaty of surrender, but she knew, with certainty, that she was looking at one now.

Her eyes flew to Sir Rowland's face, his bland smile.

'You are going to surrender!' she exclaimed. 'While Lord Devenish is sick you are going against his express orders!'

He raised a surprised eyebrow.

'Do you not *want* to be free?' he asked in genuine astonishment.

It was a pertinent question, she knew, and it was as well he did not really expect an answer, thinking he already knew it. Free, he had said. Free for what? She had been free just now in the curve of Sebastian's arm, with his lips on her hair: as free as she could ever choose to be. She bent her head now, and said nothing.

'Master Pritchard,' Sir Rowland's voice continued, 'has been sent by your brother to assure himself that Dame Farrell, and yourself and the children, are alive and well before committing his signature to the terms so far agreed. I think, Master Pritchard, that you will agree they show no sign of ill-usage, despite a long siege and a shortage of supplies. Mistress Farrell, as I said, has been occupied most charitably with nursing the wounded – hence her, shall we say, somewhat less than ordered appearance.'

Richenda raised her head to look at Master Pritchard. He was looking them over gravely, as if to satisfy himself that they were indeed as well as could be expected. The children returned his scrutiny with solemn distrust, except Elizabeth, who remembered him well: though even she had learned not to trust too readily. But on Jane's face there was only a new happiness dawning, a hope and anticipation which brought a sharp envious pain to Richenda, though she would not accept or recognise it.

'I think,' said Master Pritchard after a moment or two, 'that I can safely and with a good conscience carry news to Sir William Farrell of the wellbeing of those dearest to him. And you, sir, do we understand that you are fully empowered to agree these terms in the absence of Lord Devenish, and that your part in them will be fully implemented? That is to say, that your signature will be as binding on your party as Sir William's is on ours?'

Sir Rowland bowed his head graciously. 'You can be sure of that, Master Pritchard.'

Richenda's eyes widened, and she saw that Sir Rowland gave her a furtive glance, as if to warn her against suggesting otherwise. She was right, then, as she had thought – Lord Devenish had given him no powers to make peace.

The two men gave their attention to the document, running through the terms one by one: generous terms, such as would only be given to save the lives of precious hostages. She knew William would never have agreed them otherwise with so hated an enemy.

And then into this atmosphere of gentle-manly negotiation came an interrup-tion which was totally unexpected. The door flew open with a crash and there, swaying on his feet, his hand gripping the doorpost for support, his face white and his breath coming in choking gasps, stood Lord Devenish.

Richenda gave a cry and ran forward, but the look on his face stopped her in her tracks. He had not seen her, she knew, for one thing only had brought him here.

'Laverick!' he said hoarsely. 'There'll be no terms – not while I live. We fight on!'

And then the astonishing illusory strength which his willpower had called up to bring him here gave out, and he crumpled to the floor in a faint. Richenda came to him now, and Master Pritchard, and together they carried him to a chair. Sir Rowland came with a glass of wine, hastily poured, and handed it to Richenda with a little smile. She looked at it in astonishment, remembering even at this moment of crisis that supplies were low, that they had drunk nothing but water since the siege began.

'A little cache I found somewhere,' he explained airily, but had the grace to blush at her look of contempt.

She took the wine all the same, and held it to Sebastian's lips as he slowly regained consciousness. She was relieved to see that a faint colour came to his face, and he opened his eyes. It was a relief, too, to see that he was still strong enough for anger, and had no time to waste on any other triviality.

'If you sign that, Laverick, I shall countermand it,' he declared. 'I'm not dead yet, and the men will still follow me sooner than you. There will be no surrender. Is that clear?'

The question was addressed not only to Sir Rowland, but also to Master Pritchard, who gazed uncertainly from one to the other.

'In that case...' he began. And then Richenda intervened.

'No!' she exclaimed. 'Don't be foolish. What sense is there in fighting on? Haven't we all suffered enough?'

Lord Devenish looked at her wryly.

'"*Et tu, Brute?*"' he quoted. That hurt, for him to use the words of Julius Caesar to the friend who stabbed him; as if she too had turned against him now.

'Can't you see?' she asked imploringly. 'It is for you too I want this.'

And then she stopped. What more could she say, before them all, without betraying their love to unsympathetic eyes? And he too was silent, watching her, trying to make her understand, without words, what he could not say. At last she could bear it no longer and turned to Sir Rowland.

'Let me speak to him alone – please! I think you will not regret it.'

Sir Rowland hesitated, looking instinctively to Sebastian for guidance.

'Let her have her way. It can do no harm,' said Lord Devenish. 'But my decision is made, as it always has been.'

'Then I don't see....' began Master Pritchard again, but Sir Rowland took his arm.

'Be patient a little longer, my friend. My lord, let me help you into this room here – you can be private there.'

It was a small adjoining room containing a truckle bed, for the convenience of whoever used the office: and it was there that Sebastian took his seat on the bed, and Richenda faced him at last.

'I don't see the purpose of this,' he began obstinately.

'Well, I do,' she argued. 'How in any case did you know what was going on in there?'

'I guessed, first. From the silence of the guns, and his sending for you. Then I demanded an explanation from the first soldier I met– But that is neither here nor there, Richenda. I have no intention of coming to terms with your brother.'

'But why not?' she demanded. 'Don't you want us to be safe? You said you loved me – do you want me to have more of this to endure?'

She knew it was a feeble argument, for her

heart was not in it: she knew she could endure anything, so long as he was there. But she thought, too, that it was one argument which might sway him. She was wrong.

'I have always promised that you will be unharmed, all of you.'

'Unharmed, while you ride out to be killed by my brother?' she cried. 'Is that supposed to make me happy?'

He smiled slightly. 'I would hope not. But I see no more desirable alternative.'

'I can – that you and I come out of all this alive and well. I cannot see how you can wish for anything else.'

'Oh, come now, Richenda!' he exclaimed, his patience giving way. 'You surely are not simple enough to think there can be any future for us after this, however it ends? Either I die here now, fighting to the last – as I choose to do – or I go from here humiliated and defeated into imprisonment or exile.

'The cause I serve is doomed, Richenda, and only the disloyal can hope not to suffer the same fate. You serve another cause, and you will live on here in peace and contentment, to marry one day perhaps – some good honest Puritan landowner or a man ready to adapt his principles to suit the new colour of the times. But for you and me–' he heard his voice break on the words – 'no, Richenda, for us the past hours together were all we could ever hope for of happiness. It must be enough.'

'But it is not enough!' her heart cried defiantly, rebelliously: only she could not say it because of the dismal knell in her brain which told her he was right.

'That, my dear heart,' he went on very softly, 'is why I must fight on. Because I cannot bear to end in humiliation and defeat. You said I was proud: it is true. I would rather you remembered me for a heroic last stand – however futile – than for a tame acceptance of the end of everything.'

She knelt then at his feet, and took his hand in hers.

'Oh, why are you so blind, my love? Don't you see that it may not always be like this – there may be hope in the future, even for us. Men cannot hate for ever. One day, surely, there will be room for us all in this country to live together again in peace, and then you will come back and ... and I shall be here. I would wait a lifetime for you, Sebastian, if it came to that.'

'It is a slender chance, Richenda – and not enough. Once I had lands and wealth, all that a man could hope to offer to the woman he loves. I cannot see that I shall ever have that again, even if things go as you hope–'

'Do you think I would mind that?' she demanded fiercely.

'No, but I should.'

'Your pride again, your stupid pride!– Then let me put it another way, for the last time. You say you love me, you wish for my happiness. If you die, my love, then my happiness is over, and all my hope of happiness. There can never be anyone who means to me what you do. But so long as you are alive somewhere – in prison, in France, at the world's end, even – then I can hold one little flame of hope to treasure and guard and keep alive against the day when perhaps you will come riding up to the gate out there and find I have waited for you all along. I don't want a dead hero, Sebastian: just a living man, to love as long as there is breath in my body.'

He was silent then, his eyes on her face, reading there her deep sincerity, her love, her passionate need for him to live, at whatever cost to his pride. At last he raised his hand and laid it on her hair.

'Do you really know what you ask, Richenda?'

She nodded: 'Yes – for I too am proud, remember?'

'Then for you only, I will do it,' he said. 'As I would for no other living soul.'

CHAPTER THIRTEEN

This, then, they knew, must be their moment of parting, the last time that they could hope to be alone together. Sebastian reached down and drew her against him as she knelt at his feet by the low bed, and she clung to him with a desperate hopeless passion, as if somehow the pain and loss of the coming parting could be wiped out in the closeness of their embrace. His mouth found hers, as a thirsty man finds water, and her lips parted beneath his longing kiss, her fingers thrusting their way into the thickness of his hair to draw him closer, to make him part of herself as she ached to become one with him.

Then he was on his knees beside her, his arm so firm about her that she could scarcely breathe, his hand caressing her through the loose folds of her smock. Slowly they swayed in one long movement to the

314

floor, and the sweet intoxicating weight of his body was on her, his lips moving from her mouth, to her chin, to her throat, over the smooth skin of shoulder and breast. Her fingers twisted in his hair, holding him to her, and she surrendered wholly to the coming moment when he would surely make her his at last.

Only he did not. As he drew away she gave a little moan and tried to bring him back to her again, but he said hoarsely, 'No, my dear heart – not this way. I love you too much to shame you now. One day – one day, if I ever come back and make you my wife–'

She got up slowly, and moved alongside him where he sat on the floor with his back resting against the bed.

'I don't think I can bear it,' she said.

He caressed her cheek tenderly with his strong brown fingers.

'If I can bear it, then so can you,' he said. 'We have no choice. Either way we will be parted; but as you said, by taking your way perhaps we have some hope that some day we can meet again. And now we have been alone here long enough: they'll be wondering what's become of us.'

He kissed her lightly, gently, on the mouth: his eyes were sombre now. 'Let's get it over with. And remember always, whatever happens, that I love you.'

She rose to help him to his feet and together they went to tell the others of his decision.

She guessed what it must have cost Sebastian then to take his seat at the table and put his ungainly left-handed signature to the treaty of surrender, under Sir Rowland Laverick's triumphant gaze. She watched his face as he wrote, the withdrawn expression, the bleak eyes, and thought it hard that he should have this to face when he had already suffered so much. And it was only the first cruel step in the acceptance of defeat which she had forced on him – there would be worse to come.

When it was done he looked up, and became at once calm, assured, in full control.

'Right,' he said to Sir Rowland, 'I'm resuming my command, Laverick. You may escort Master Pritchard to the gate, and then I shall have certain matters to discuss, if we're to be ready to march out at ten tomorrow. You, madam, and Mistress Farrell and the children may return to your rooms: I imagine you will have preparations to make. Harry here will escort you.'

Not even a glance in her direction: the brisk manner excluded her completely, finally, told her as no words could do that it was over.

Numb with misery, choking on the painful aching lump in her throat, Richenda followed blindly after the others to their rooms. Her own room at last: she should have been pleased.

At the door, as their escort left them, Jane asked: 'What was all that about in there? What did you say to make Lord Devenish change his mind?'

Richenda shrugged, and could find no words. The tears were pricking her eyelids, and she longed for the privacy of her room. But Jane must have an answer, if she were not to guess something of the truth. She cleared her throat, and said, 'I ... knew something ... something he hadn't thought of.'

Even now her voice sounded strained, unlike its usual sweet light tones. But before Jane could question her further, she fled to the sanctuary of her room.

'Whatever happens ... I love you.' What use was that, now? What possible use, what possible comfort? Tomorrow she must watch him march out with his men – not for a last desperate battle, for that at least she must be thankful – but there was small enough comfort in it. He would go from her life, just as she had learned to love, just as she had found that love returned, and take all the brightness with him.

If only she'd known sooner what she felt; known when he was just Daniel Bridge the falconer, who saved her life: then they would have had longer together. But then perhaps it might even have been worse, to part like this, though she could not believe that anything could be worse than this pain which was tearing her in pieces.

She had told him that by marching to safety tomorrow it would give them some future hope of happiness. But those lightly spoken words had turned to ashes now, grey and cheerless, empty of life.

'I shall never see him again,' she thought. 'I have lived my life, I have known all the joy it can offer. It is over now, and I must learn to go on alone in the shadow of that little happiness.'

The tears came then, pouring out in harsh bitter sobs which brought no comfort and no relief.

It was Nurse who came to her at last, clicking her tongue in affectionate concern as she crossed the room.

'Now then, my chick, this won't do – this won't do at all!'

She took Richenda in her arms, as if she were still a small child needing comfort, and patted her back soothingly. 'We'll all have to make the best of it, my lass,' she went on. 'These things happen, and there's nothing we can do. But if you want to keep clear of awkward questions, you'll have to dry those tears and put on a brighter face for us all – Come now, your brother sent in a real feast with Master Pritchard, and they're all sitting down to it next door – and they were all set to come for you when I said I'd go – I guessed how it would be with you, my chick. Come on, then – and let me say that one day you'll be giving thanks that it did end like this. He's not good enough for you, not half good enough–'

'You don't know him!' exclaimed Richenda through her tears.

'I'd have thought I knew him as well as you do – but there, let it go. You'll get over it, even if it doesn't seem like it just now. And tomorrow your brother will be home and we'll all be happy again just as we were – and all this will seem like a bad dream.'

Richenda could not find the strength to argue. She dried her eyes and blew her nose and followed Nurse without a word into Jane's room.

'It's all been a bit much for Mistress Richenda,' Nurse explained as they went in. 'On top of everything, all the excitement. A good night's rest is what she needs – and this feast, of course.'

For it was indeed a feast: food such as they had only dreamed of over the past weeks. Venison pasties, crisp and golden, and apple tarts, jellies and syllabubs and glowing red wine: it should have been able to tempt even Richenda to eat, if anything could, but she could only think that it was hard to enjoy these delicacies when Lord Devenish must still be faced with the inevitable bread and cheese – even if there would be more of it, now that there was no longer a need to conserve supplies.

She was glad at least that the joyous excitement of the others made them oblivious to her own silence, once Nurse had given her explanation. The talk and laughter washed around her, though a few small things caught in her brain, scarcely noticed. Nurse had been sent to join them, she gathered, for only one man was unfit to march out tomorrow, and Nell was to stay behind to look after him, according to the terms of the treaty. Everywhere was in a bustle, Nurse said, as the soldiers made ready to leave – and quieter than for a long time, since they had nothing to be cheerful about in defeat.

Jane, for her part, had enjoyed a happy talk with Master Pritchard. From him she had learned that for all the heavy bombardment there was little serious damage to the castle. William had trained his guns on the points where he could most easily hurt the enemy soldiers, having watched with care to learn where those were. He had known well enough that it would take months to destroy the castle sufficiently to force a surrender, and involve too much risk to the hostages held inside.

Richenda was thankful when at last Nurse felt she could take her leave of them and go to bed. But there was little comfort for her any longer in Nurse's soothing talk, now that she knew what the old woman thought of her love. It did not help to have her make nothing of it, to belittle it with the assurance that she would soon get over it.

And she knew when she lay alone at last that it was not true. It was as if she had waited all her life to meet Sebastian, restless, bored, unsatisfied until he put his arm about her and told her he loved her. At that moment she had known that her life had found its purpose and its centre, that she had found the other half of herself.

And now she was torn in two again,

wrenched from him by the cruel accident of war – though that same accident had also brought them together. Tomorrow she would watch him go, if she could bear it; and then she must be ready, smiling and calm, to greet the return of her brother as she ought.

She had seen in Jane's face, and in her voice, and in the laughter of the children – even in Nurse's smiles – what it would mean to them. It ought, after all, to bring her some joy too. There would be rejoicing such as they had never known before, she was sure: feasting, the delayed ceremony of Jeremy's breeching – the small doublet and shirt and breeches had long been ready, laid aside in the clothes-press in Jane's room.

And later, when things were normal again there would be rides and walks and visits, hunting and hawking, journeys to market and church, all the ordinary pleasures of everyday life which had for so long been denied to them. How could she be anything but happy?

How could she be happy ever again? she thought. The quiet orderly tediousness of life would return, full of affection and friendliness and comfort; but there would be no passion, no excitement, nothing even to look forward to. Perhaps she would be proved right in the hope she had held out to Sebastian, that one day he would come back. But it would not, could not be soon: the bitterness of civil war went too deep for that. Meanwhile she would grow older, lose her beauty perhaps, and her enthusiasm for life, even, worse still, her courage.

William and Jane would not mind if she did not marry, she thought; would be happy to let her live here with them. But she would never quite be at home as they were. It would be William's home she would help to run, William's guests she would greet at the door, William's children who would grow before her eyes. Never, never her own – and his. And if he ever came back might it not be too late then to bear his children, too late for anything but to share an old age uncheered by memories of a lifetime lived in each other's company?

The night passed and Richenda did not sleep, kept wakeful by the yearning sadness of her thoughts. She watched the moon rise and flood her room with stark silver light, and fade again with the dawn. And it was as the castle woke to life in that early greyness that she knew with certainty that her courage was not great enough to take her through the empty years which lay ahead. For her there must be another way.

She rose and dressed in a simple gown of light blue homespun, and rolled her few small essential possessions in a spare neckerchief, tying it firmly on top; pulled her cloak about her, and went in search of Jane.

They were already up and dressed, the children dancing about the room, wild with excitement, despite Nurse's laughing remonstrances, Jane at the mirror in her best amber gown brushing her brown hair until it shone as brightly as did her eyes. She looked like a girl again, preparing to welcome her lover. Richenda was almost sorry that she must shatter that transparent joy, however briefly.

Jane turned, smiling, and then a little puzzled frown replaced the smile. 'Where are you going? You can't go out yet, not until William's here. The garrison must march out first – and that's not for hours yet.'

'I'm going with them,' said Richenda, her voice hushed by the frightened beating of her heart. Jane dropped her brush.

'What did you say?'

'I said, I am going with them – with him, with my lord.'

For long moments Jane stood motionless, speechless, unable to understand. Then she whispered, 'Going with him? With Lord Devenish? What are you talking about? It's over now, he can't make you do what you don't want to do.'

'It is not what I don't want to do,' said Richenda with a lift of the head. 'I would go to the world's end with him.'

She could see the panic flooding Jane's eyes.

'But you hate him!'

'You didn't see them together down in that hall, when he was sick,' Nurse broke in grimly.

Jane glanced at her, and back again, trying to make sense of it all. 'I think you've gone mad!' she said.

Richenda smiled suddenly and briefly.

'Perhaps,' she agreed, 'I don't know. But it's what I want – if ... if he'll have me.'

Her heart beat suddenly faster than ever at the thought: she had not considered that possibility.

Jane came to her and took her hands, her tone urgent, imploring. 'Richenda, you can't have thought it over properly.'

'I've been thinking about nothing else all night.'

'No, wait a moment. Fair enough, you love him – I can't see why for the life of me, but if it's so, then that's that. In time of peace, if things were normal, then he could come and ask William for your hand and be considered on his merits – and if he had means enough, as he did once, I suppose, and you really loved him, then I suppose there might be some small chance William would consent. And that you wouldn't regret it afterwards.

'But it's not like that, one bit. He's our enemy, and we're at war, and now it is nearly over, and at the very best he will have to go into exile, and he will have nothing left with which to keep a wife. Go with him now and you will go hungry and homeless and never taste good food or enjoy new clothes or have any of the comforts you have known all your life until now.

'It will be like that dreadful time when we escaped, only worse, much worse, because it may never come to an end as long as you live. And you won't have people you love for company, except for him, I suppose – only rough soldiers and the camp women–'

'My friends,' Richenda said proudly, remembering those who had worked at her side in the hall.

'But not what you are used to. And you'll be one of them, Richenda, remember that!' added Jane, more forcefully still. 'Think, dear, think hard. You love him and trust him, but what if he betrays your trust? What if you march out with him and he seduces you, and then abandons you somewhere far away? It could happen–'

'Never!' said Richenda. 'He would never do that!'

'And,' Jane went on remorselessly, 'there is

William. Do you think he's going to sit by quietly while you ride out under his nose with his most deadly enemy?'

Richenda had not thought of that: it struck her like a blow, crushing her new hope, and she sank on to a stool, her head bent. She could see it only too clearly. William rushing to save her, imagining she had been compelled to go; fighting Sebastian, very likely killing him, disabled as he was. And she unable to explain, until afterwards—

And even if she could explain somehow, William, like Jane, would never understand, and he had it in his power to prevent her going.

Then she had a new idea. She raised her head, to destroy the short-lived satisfaction in Jane's face.

'I shall go in disguise, somehow. Sebastian will know what to do. And I'll leave a letter with you for William, telling him what I have done, and why – only you must not give it to him until tomorrow, until we've had time to get away – and you mustn't tell him anything either until then. I know it will be hard, but you can, I'm sure you can.'

She stood up. 'Jane, I know exactly what I shall face with him: I am young, I know, and often foolish, but not so foolish as to walk into this with my eyes closed. I am sure, very sure, that this is what I must do, and nothing else.'

Even then, it took Jane a long time to accept that no argument would move her sister-in-law. She gave up in the end more from weariness than from any realisation that she could do nothing else. It was almost nine o'clock when Richenda went at last to write her letter to William, pouring into it all her love for Sebastian, all her trust in him, everything she could to make William understand: and asking him, very humbly, to forgive her for the pain and distress she caused to him and to Jane. And then she went to give it to Jane, and to say goodbye.

The children took her departure without a great deal of interest. They were too excited at their father's coming to mind very much. Which, Richenda thought, was just as well: she was only sorry Jane and William would not be able to take it so philosophically. Or

Nurse, who shook her head sadly.

Jane embraced her with tears in her eyes, and promised most carefully to carry out her instructions concerning the letter.

'If–' Richenda said hesitantly, 'if Sebastian won't have me, I'll ask for it back.'

'I only hope he won't,' Jane said without conviction, and then she added, very slowly and gently, 'Richenda, you know, don't you, that whatever happens there'll always be a place for you here? Whatever you've done, you will be welcome back.'

'I know,' Richenda said huskily, 'and thank you.'

And then she ran from the room before she should cry and lead them to think she had changed her mind.

He was sitting in his room when she reached it, splendid in the scarlet coat he had worn that triumphant night in the hall, his dark hair – longer now – combed and shining; and struggling, one-handed, to pull on his gleaming boots. He was also pale and weary, his face set in stern lines, which did not soften as he turned and saw her.

'What are you doing–? Richenda, this makes it no easier–'

Ignoring his question, she laid down her bundle and came to help him with his boots, kneeling at his feet.

'You shouldn't really be out of bed you know,' she said with affectionate disapproval.

'I'm not going through the additional humiliation of being dragged out of here on a wagon, Richenda. You should know that.'

'You can lean on me then,' she said. 'I'll be at your side.'

'Mm,' he said absent-mindedly, pushing his foot into the second boot. And then, sharply: 'What did you say?'

She sat back on her heels and looked up at him, and her heart did a double somersault as those dark grey eyes met hers.

'I am coming with you,' she whispered, 'if you will have me.'

Sebastian said nothing, though she saw the faint colour drain from his face and then slowly return. She felt his hand close over hers as it lay imploringly on his knee.

She said: 'I want to share your poverty and

your hunger and your loneliness. I want to be with you always, through good and ill, whatever becomes of us. I want to turn my back on all the quiet dull comfortable things I have always known and come with you wherever you lead me, whatever it costs. And I know it will not be easy: only that it is what I want to do, above everything. If you will have me.'

He spoke then, softly, his voice rough with emotion. 'If I will have you– Oh, Richenda!' and he raised her into his arms, to meet his kiss.

There was not much time, and there was the problem of William. Sebastian had a solution to that, as she knew he would: a doublet and breeches, stockings and shirt and shoes from a dead soldier, a lad about her size. And a hat to conceal her hair, hastily pinned out of sight on top of her head; and last of all a smudge or two of soot from the hearth, hastily applied to her face to complete the disguise.

He stood back to look at her afterwards, and laughed.

'What a disreputable urchin, my love!–

Now, bundle up that gown into your parcel there. It can go in my pack – you can put it on as soon as we're well away from here. And then we'll find a parson to marry us, and it will be your wedding gown.'

Richenda's face shone through the dirt, and he held out his arm for her to run into his embrace.

'I'll dirty all your proud finery,' she said. But he did not seem to care, risking a kiss in spite of it.

It was her turn to help him then, buckling on his sword, tying his sash, pulling his velvet cloak about him.

'There'll be a horse for you,' he said as her fingers were busy. 'A good quiet one.'

'I'll ride Bluebell,' she suggested, with a sweet sidelong smile.

'You'll do nothing of the kind,' he said, as she knew he would. 'She's a vicious brute at the best of times, but with precious little exercise – no!'

'Yes, dear,' she agreed meekly.

'If only,' he retorted, 'I could hope you would always be as dutiful!'

'But wouldn't that be tedious, my love?'

He laid his hand over hers then, the sparkle gone from his eyes.

'Richenda, you said once that whatever terms he agreed, your brother would not see me go free – I don't want to put you at risk.'

She blushed a little.

'That was said in anger, my darling. William is an honourable man, he would never break his word. But I ... I wanted to hurt you then–'

He shook his head. 'What have I done, to saddle myself for life with such a sharp – tongued wench?'

'It was only because I loved you so,' she said obscurely.

He laughed then in pure delight, and kissed her.

'Oh, my darling, it's as well I know exactly what you mean!'

And then they were ready, and there was no more room for laughter. Down to the courtyard, where a horse was somehow found for her, and she mounted under the curious stares of the men; and waited quietly while Sebastian gave the orders for the march. Briskly, unemotionally, as if she were indeed only one of his soldiers, he ordered her into the ranks behind him.

The portcullis was raised, the drawbridge slowly lowered. She heard his voice, clear in the sudden quiet, ringing out the command to advance.

A mournful roll on the drums; and they moved forward, under the archway, over the drawbridge, on to the sunlit grass, where William watched unsuspecting as his sister rode out with joy in her heart, and her eyes on the proud figure of the man she loved.